# THE BOOK OF DUELS

# THE BOOK OF DUELS

Michael Garriga
Illustrations by Tynan Kerr

milkweed
editions

Published 2014 by Milkweed Editions
Printed in Canada
Cover design by Rebecca Lown
Cover illustration by Tynan Kerr
Interior illustrations by Tynan Kerr and Megan Garriga

14 15 16 17 18   5 4 3 2 1
*First Edition*

3 1969 02243 7825

Milkweed Editions, an independent nonprofit publisher, gratefully acknowledges sustaining support from the Bush Foundation; the Patrick and Aimee Butler Foundation; the Driscoll Foundation; the Jerome Foundation; the Lindquist & Vennum Foundation; the McKnight Foundation; the National Endowment for the Arts; the Target Foundation; and other generous contributions from foundations, corporations, and individuals. Also, this activity is made possible by the voters of Minnesota through a Minnesota State Arts Board Operating Support grant, thanks to a legislative appropriation from the arts and cultural heritage fund, and a grant from the Wells Fargo Foundation Minnesota. For a full listing of Milkweed Editions supporters, please visit www.milkweed.org.

Library of Congress Cataloging-in-Publication Data

Garriga, Michael Christopher, 1971–
    [Prose works. Selections]
    The book of duels / Michael Garriga ; illustrations by Tynan Kerr. — First Edition.
      pages    cm
    ISBN 978-1-57131-093-4 (acid-free paper) — ISBN 978-1-57131-886-2 (ebook)
    I. Kerr, Tynan, ill. II. Title.
    PS3607.A77335A6 2014
    813'.6—dc23
                                                        2013043097

Milkweed Editions is committed to ecological stewardship. We strive to align our book production practices with this principle, and to reduce the impact of our operations in the environment. We are a member of the Green Press Initiative, a nonprofit coalition of publishers, manufacturers, and authors working to protect the world's endangered forests and conserve natural resources. *The Book of Duels* was printed on acid-free 100% postconsumer-waste paper by Friesens Corporation.

For Robert Olen Butler

# Table of Contents

## PART I: OFFENSE

## PART II: CHALLENGE

# PART III: SATISFACTION

When challenged to a duel, do much or nothing at all.

— Casanova, *The Duel* (paraphrase)

"Duels were demonstrations of manner, not marksmanship;
they were intricate games of dare and counterdare, ritualized
displays of bravery, military prowess, and—above all—willingness
to sacrifice one's life for one's honor. A man's response to the
*threat* of gunplay bore far more meaning than the exchange of
fire itself."

— Joanne B. Freeman, *Affairs of Honor*

In one of the most famous duels of early New Orleans,
Bernard Marigny challenged James Humble, a Georgian who
stood almost seven feet tall, to a duel. Humble told a trusted
friend, "I will not fight him. I know nothing of this dueling
business."

"You must," his friend protested. "No gentleman can refuse
a challenge."

"I'm not a gentleman," Humble retorted. "I'm only a
blacksmith."

Humble was assured that he would be ruined socially if he
declined to meet the challenge of the Creole, who was a crack
shot and noted swordsman. However, his friend pointed out
that as the challenged man, the blacksmith had the choice of
weapons and could so choose to put himself on equal terms
with his adversary. Humble considered the matter for a day or
two and then sent this reply to Marigny: "I accept your challenge, and in the exercise of my privilege, I stipulate that the
duel shall take place in Lake Pontchartrain in six feet of water,
sledgehammers to be used as weapons."

Since Marigny was less than five feet and eight inches
tall, and so slight that he could scarcely lift a sledgehammer,
this was giving Humble an equal chance with a vengeance.
Marigny's friends urged him to stand on a box and run the
risk of having his skull cracked by the huge blacksmith's

hammer, but Marigny declared it impossible for himself to fight a man with such a fine sense of humor. Instead he apologized to Humble, and the two became firm friends.

— Herbert Asbury, *The French Quarter* (paraphrase)

Inspired by movie gunfights, Nobel Prize–winning physicist Niels Bohr first suggested the intentional act of drawing and shooting is slower to execute than the reactive response. He once did an impromptu research project to find out why good guys in movies always win quick-draw duels. After many mock gunfights in university hallways with graduate students, Bohr concluded the villain always tries to draw his gun first (and so must consciously move his hands), while the hero always reacts and draws by reflex as soon as he sees the villain moving. There is good evidence from imaging scans that our brain system uses different messaging routes depending on intentional and reactive movements, but this is the first time the two speeds of thought have been calculated.

— Welchman, et al., "The Quick and the Dead" (paraphrase)

"I, being a citizen of this State, have not fought a duel with deadly weapons within this State nor out of it, nor have I sent or accepted a challenge to fight a duel with deadly weapons, nor have I acted as second in carrying a challenge, nor aided or assisted any person thus offending, so help me God."

— Current oath of office for Kentucky State officeholders

To avert an all-out war, the vice president of Iraq, Taha Yassin Ramadan, suggested the following on October 2, 2002: "The American president should specify a group and we will specify a group and choose neutral ground, with Kofi Annan as referee and use one weapon with a president [Saddam Hussein] against a president [George W. Bush],

a vice president against a vice president, and a minister
against a minister in a duel."

— Associated Press

"In the freshly minted United States of America, the punish-
able-by-dissection category was extended to include duelists,
the death sentence clearly not posing much of a deterrent to
the type of fellow who agrees to settle his differences by the
dueling pistol."

— Mary Roach, *Stiff: The Curious Lives of Human Cadavers*

"Some people stop living long before they die."

— Drive-By Truckers, "The Living Bubba"

"I thoroughly disapprove of duels. I consider them unwise and
I know they are dangerous. Also, sinful. If a man should challenge me now, I would go to that man and take him kindly and
forgivingly by the hand and lead him to a quiet retired spot,
and *kill* him."

— Mark Twain, *The Autobiography of Mark Twain*

"On February 5, 1897, Marcel Proust challenged the liter-
ary critic Jean Lorrain to a duel after the latter, a homosexual
himself, alluded to Proust's sexual affair with a man of means,
suggesting this was how his novel *Pleasures and Days* came to be
published. Both men fired shots and missed and, in this manner, Proust's honor was restored. It has been apocryphally
noted that, years later, Proust would say that when he fired his
pistol, the smell of the gun smoke was so strong, it sent a series
of flashes roiling through his brain to an ultimate moment
when, as a child, he'd first sat in front of an open fire eating,
but what else, a madeleine."

— Michael Garriga

"Those are people who died, died / They were all my friends, and they died."

— Jim Carroll Band, "People Who Died"

"Another study found only one duelist in fourteen died. Most duelists escaped unscathed, or with minor wounds, at worst. It had become fashionable among some writers to portray these affairs as more farcical than fatal."

— Thomas Fleming, *The Duel: Alexander Hamilton, Aaron Burr, and the Future of America*

# THE BOOK OF DUELS

# PART I: †OFFENSE

# Slouching toward the Land of Nod:
# Abel v. Cain

*Just East of Eden,*
*Once upon a Time*

## Abel, 17, Shepherd

How easy it must be to sit beside a fig tree and let the wind turn your soil and the rain bury your seed and the sun pull your wheat and bean from the field, while here I hold a lonely vigil, watch over the hillside speckled by sheep, wary as ever of hound and hawk, because even though the lion may once have lain with the lamb, as Mother always says, it now devours them as prey—yesterday, I witnessed three lionesses bring down a gazelle and tear its flesh from the bone—it is little wonder to me why Holy Father loved my offering more than his, but not Mother, never Mother—she who loves Cain more than me, loves Cain more than Father, loves Cain indeed more than Holy Father—she strokes his hair and hums as she eats his lavash and lentils and ignores the cheese and yogurt I bring to our table—sometimes in the heat of early morn I smell her in the lambs' wool as I milk them—last night I dreamt I took a wee one by his hind feet— him jerking and bleating 'gainst the sweat of my arms and chest and I held him up to the heavens and sank my teeth into his throat, the first man ever to taste blood, instead of the flesh of berry and herb and grain—I tore his muscle loose from bone and my jaw ached from the chewing, and when I woke, I ached still and so slaughtered a firstling and rendered his fat and brought it unto the Lord, Who smiled and said it was good, and if it was good enough for Him, then why not for me as well?

I herd my sheep toward his field and my strange brother, tall and gangly and talking to himself, cries unto me, *Your sheep are eating the crops and they are drinking the needed water,* and I say, *Shut up, shut up, shut up, you goddamn bleating baby,* and I shove him hard and he falls to all fours and I jump on his back and oh it feels good to spit the khat from my mouth and drive my teeth into his neck.

## Cain, 19, Farmer

With the wind in my teeth I howl the first poetry of the world and call each unnamed and new experience the thing it shall be called and I bring forth from the very earth the fruit of my labor conjured so by song—and so it is and so it is good—and I break the earth that God hath made and I plant the seed that God hath given unto me and I adore the sun and I adore the rain and I adore the wind and cry: *You, you shall be called* emmer *and you shall be* fava *and you,* barley, *and this the* scythe *and that the* harvest, and I will continue so, even as God shuns my offering and even as my brother turns on me and pushes me into the earth where I spin and smash his head, over and over, until he lies in the dirt and there he dies and I call it *murder.*

As I stand in the sun, the flint blade still red in my hand, my own blood runs down my neck and soaks my tunic and my brother's blood seeps into the mouth of mother earth and my dark skin begins to throb and brighten and glow an ungodly white and I hear His voice again, *There is thy mark upon thee, Cain, for all to know thee by thy deed.*

# God, Eternal Witness

# Children of the Sun: Musashi v. Kojiro

*On the Island of Funajima, Japan,*
*April 13, 1612*

Ah, summer grasses! All that remain of the warrior's dream.

~ Matsuo Bashō

## Miyamoto Musashi, 28,
## Ronin & Future Author of *The Book of Five Rings*

My katana cut through his kimono and armor and flesh and when he dropped his steel I turned to the boat and motioned for my team to leave—his seconds surely would have killed us all—and we've timed it just so, the tide pulling us out as we paddle steady with the waves, the salt in my beard and the wind in my dress, and we rise and fall with the water, we rise and fall, and the sea carries me back to my village where I am a child, the snow falling softly outside, and I sit with my legs beneath the *kotatsu*, the coals warming me, and I am crying in my mother's arms—she squats next to me and strokes my back and says, *Shhhh, Saru-chan, shhhh,* as I try to describe the dream I've just had of sitting by a pond whose surface is covered with lotus leaves, in the middle of which is but one lone bloom, orange and pink and far removed, and I reach for it with tiny fingers and I am stretched long and thin and then topple and splash into the water, beneath whose surface all is darkness and dry, and though I know my father was killed in the Battle of Sekigahara, he now stands before me in a doorway, his hand reaches out to me, yet the closer I move, the tinier he becomes and so I stand still as a mountain and stare for a long long time calling to him, *Tousan! Tousan!* until he fades into an ultimate light and vanishes, yet I cannot find the words to tell her this, like a flower that blooms at night can never wish for a thing as miraculous and needed as the sun.

I wake on the boat, the wind blowing us to our destination,

and I remember another dream in which I was a warrior who'd been slain in a duel, though perhaps that was no dream—perhaps I am truly the dead man and this voyage but my final dream.

## Sasaki Kojiro, 27,
## Samurai & Founder of the *Kenjutsu* School

The heavy rain has soaked my robes and it weighs down my
body and my blood is leaving me and so I sit in the moist
sand and watch my footprints fill with water, my life being erased
one drop at a time, and when I am gone who will remember the
things I've seen—as a child in my father's orchard, an albino fox
in the branches of a cherry tree, its pink blossoms hiding all but
his eyes and we stared at each other motionless till the sun quit
the sky; in a still body of water, two snakes gripping a carp in their
mouths, one by its tail and one by its head, the three joined into
a new self-devouring creature; in Master Toda Seigen's dojo, him
tossing, like a sumo, a handful of purifying salt and catching each
grain on the flat blade of his *nodachi*—and I know I will die now
on this island and I try to stay calm, relax my mind, and let my
spirit leave this crude vessel, but we all in our folly think we will
live more years—even an old man on his deathbed can believe he
has ten more—but my days are through and only my foolish pride,
and the many years preceding this very last day, have allowed me
to believe that tomorrow was ever offered, because there is, of
course, no tomorrow—there is only this moment—I recline to my
elbow and, with my last strength, lower myself flat and cross my
hands over my chest, listen to my own breath become the crashing waves, open my mouth to catch one last drop of this world,
acknowledge the weak and thankless sun, a dull white hole burned
in the gray sky, and close my eyes forever.

Master Lee, 23,
Tanka Poet & Disciple of Sasaki Kojiro
(with apologies for the poor translation)

Cherry blossoms in full bloom—
Sunrise above water burns high—
man and fruit to fall too soon

at Noon, pale sun sits on high—
challenge! duel!—both day and we await

near Sunset he arrives, disheveled, late, insulting—
I say not his name—
look: wind in robes like dragon wings

mad, my master overplays his hand—
blood red as Sunset, as cherries

my world upended—rat kills cat—
I shall never follow another—
what use: world, water, fire, wind, void?

Yet still gull cries beyond me
Yet still pages set before me

Dusk comes, steals away our light—sun sets—
Darkness, moon has failed us—
what is left to do but weep?

Shall I now seek revenge for him?
Shall I suicide or use my pen?

# First-Called Quits: Pelham v. Vanderhosen

*In a Whip Fight for Honor near Lynchburg, Virginia,*
*June 24, 1798*

## Josiah Pelham, 49,
## Owner of Pelham's Acres

Returned my boy, Brossie, all bloody and beaten, his back sprung open like a deep-bit plum, stains on the split muslin of his shirt, which I bought for him not two months ago—had gall enough to say to me, *Your boy wouldn't work, so I put the whip to his hide and you ought to as well, God's truth be known*—like that was that and he'd drop the whole affair— had he hurt one of my younguns, I'd have shot him down, dog dead, and dared any man find me guilty, but Brossie is a slave who will be beaten again, yet he is a good boy— groomed and behaved, understands what I teach, and owns manners and looks to make a white man proud—I knew his mother too, gone now a dozen years, whom I'd have set free if the law had allowed—because this man had not driven his own workers—the tobacco flowers were starting to bloom, their seeds like sand soon to drop and so to sully the soil for next year's crop—he came begging my help, so I sent him Brossie to top the tobacco—loaned him for free, no less—this simpleton thrashed the child for not working fast enough, insulting me twofold—harming my property and then my pride—so it has come to this: our left wrists bound each to each by hemp, a seven-foot length of leather in our rights, and I look him hard right square in his eyes and they drop to the dirt where I intend to bury this whelp like I would any man who'd split my mule's frog or burned down my damn barn.

My ears go a-ringing like funeral bells as the overseer calls the rules, though come swinging time I'll pop his hide and tear it clean from the muscle, like scraping a scalded hog, and no matter the rules, I'll not call quits nor hear them neither until I am satisfied.

# Luke Vanderhosen, 34,
## Foreman on the Welcome Home Plantation

Darkie wouldn't work, so damn straight I lashed him,
same as I would any brute beast of the field and now
comes riding up this great puff of smoke, nostrils flared like
a thrusting bull in rut—him with his long coat in this hot heat
to hide his pistol I suppose; him who's fathered a slew of
slave bastards; him come to slap my face and challenge me to a
fight of first-called quits, like I ain't never been beat before—
Daddy was twice the man he is and he whipped me right as
rain. There and then in front of the other foremen and slaves
I answered him true—clenched my jaw and hacked and spat
between his leather boots, pulled my hair back in a twist tail,
stuck my hand forward, and let Overseer Reagan tie us off
like you'd do any horse lathered at a drinking trough, and I
gripped the bullwhip's handle, rocked its tip dancing back and
forth—its etched handle branding my palm and my knuckles
a burning white—I seen in his eyes then that same hell-bent
horror of the mama cow that run me down when I was but a
child and me trying to doctor her sickly calf—that heifer I later
shot out of spite and Daddy beat hell out of me then too—
Reagan's steady talking but all I recall is that bawling cow and
the crush of her hooves against my ribs and the first release of
my seed as I thought I had died, unable to breathe—of a sudden, I whiff the sweet wang of skunk spray on the wind—Lord
God, I hope that ain't the last thing I smell on Your green
earth—and my damp nape goes cold.

Pelham punches my throat and I spin and gasp and fall to

a knee—flame spreads across my back and I try to scream but nothing comes—he beats my calves and he beats my neck and I can't muster the breath to call quits, and turning, I see in his eyes that it does not matter if I ever do.

# Brossie, 14,
## Slave on Pelham's Acres

Standing behind Mr. Reagan, yellow stains on his white-
collar shirt, I hold horse reins and move dirt with my
toe till the iron and 'bacco rise up to my nose but Marse say,
*Don't look away, boy, this is justice,* and just this morning as I limp
past him, Marse wretch down and catch my arm and heft
me up on back of his horse and we thunder off—wind dries
the tears and sweat from my fresh-scab skin—we get to the
Welcome Home and straightaway I point out that bully fore-
man, and Marse, he hop down and slap fire from bully's thin
lips, and they tie theyselves with a rope long enough to bind
you to a tree as they take your mama away while you cry her
name on New Year's Day—next I know that bully chokes, noise
like spurs been put to his side—and when Marse steps back and
lashes that whip, something deep below my belly rises—again
that whip sings through the air and his shirt dances off his
back and he makes a face like some catfish come ashore, with
just his eyes Mr. Reagan holds back the other foremen—the
black men, all funky from the fields, don't dare watch but they
listen and hunch each time that whip snaps, as if it was a snake
in a tree, striking—I've never seen a white man beat but just
then, holding them reins jelly-jar tight, my palms start to itch
to hold that thicker leather, to hear it creak against my fingers,
but who I got to beat—the foremen, those slaves, this bully?
Myself, I reckon this thrashing's a thing Marse gotta do but not
on me—he ain't belt me but once and even then like a father
might a son—now bully's shirt come off his skin in sopped
rags—white cloth and white skin gone to a boiling red—he lay

flat to the ground, still as a rock, save the skin on his back that opens like a wild weeping flower.

I know if he could live long enough, the scars would heal like great stalks of lightning come frayed and burnt beneath his skin, but he will not survive, so the foremen start to yell the slaves back to work and they obey but tonight they will dance and sing—Mr. Reagan, silent as an undertaker, puts his hand on Marse's sweaty shoulder, who stares at me like some raging bull, breath heaving, and me staring right back with aching palms and desires I can't yet name.

# Founding Fathers: Hamilton v. Burr

*Settling an Old Score, Weehawken, New Jersey,*
*July 11, 1804*

## General Alexander Hamilton, 49,
## Former Secretary of the US Treasury

On the walls of Fame I have penned my name in a hand indelible and swift—the Federalist Papers, the Bank of New York, the US Mint—for all the good I've given to Country, I have been persecuted from all sides—my boots sink in the sludge of this loose shore and we slog our way up the hill to where I shall engage Burr—the ignominy of Adams's rebuffs, that rascal Jefferson's uphiked nose, and even my own Federalists, pitching their tents with this devil who awaits me today, patient as a spider—I must admit, I choked his bid for governor, but now as I achieve the trail head, sweat beading on my hairline, I see him again—the burr in my side, the thorn in my eye—I fear our nation will fall asunder, capitulated by shortsighted men such as this Burr and the weakboys who'd willingly give Napoleon back his Louisiana—what's next, the whole of our country?—foreign armies sit to both the west and south and we have no standing force to fight—I shake Burr's hand and accept the pistol offered, which is heavier than I'd presumed, and I'll say this much for him: he's the only man in my life as reliable as George, my Washington, who never disappointed me save when he refused to be our king, and when I'd lift my chin to see up into his blue eyes, I'd become a child again, an orphan in the West Indies whose father had abandoned him, a boy whose mother succumbed to fever, and I would stand on the cliffs of St. Croix, the water lashing far below me, shouting straight into the wind between my cupped hands, *Daddy, Daddy*, and the wind would blow my words to shreds and dry the tears on my boyhood cheeks—

Now I've accepted Jesus Christ into my heart, though He comes and goes—so much on His mind, I suppose one cannot blame Him—how to concentrate on any single one thing—still, He's filled my heart and I will waste my first shot but thereafter I am Christ-bound to defend myself—standing twenty-five feet from this filthy Catiline, I burrow my feet in the pebbles and I slip and the hair trigger goes off and I'm not afforded the dignity of *delope*—has the Lord forsaken me too?—Burr fires his ball and a full lifetime ticks by before it burrs into my body, and in that eternity, I realize that we are a two-sided coin flipped by Fate and here I land facedown and forlorn and I forgive him everything.

# Colonel Aaron Burr, 48,
## Vice President of the United States

Last night before a hardwood fire, shivering with ague
beneath a mound of blankets and scarves, I wrote letters of address to my loved ones, none more so than sweet
Theodosia, *You are a diamond of the first water, my dear*—poor half
orphan these last ten years, I regret betrothing you to that
planter, but we will need his votes when I ascend, though if
I die first, please flee, hie away from those men who bring
themselves low by pressing slaves to service—I penned my will
only to realize I am broke, in debt to my waistcoat—all those
books for my daughter and wine for myself and glorious
Richmond Hill—I see Hamilton level his pistol and so too do I
and I should have killed this Creole thirty years ago, this scamp
who has cast aspersions before my Honor—alas, he has crossed
me once too often and now it has appeared in print that he
has called me *despicable*, then had gall enough to describe its
nuanced meanings as if I'm not his equal in the world of
ideas: he is a coward at heart and I demanded his explanation,
because one way or the other I must be done with him, and
so we've come to this jag of land where we stand in plain sight
of The City and on the precipice of violating a law I'm duty-
sworn to uphold or become this nation's bona fide Bonaparte,
which I, American aristocrat, was born to be—I have liver and
stones enough to make this land mine, the whole damned
country, and since Jefferson's dropped me from the ticket
and New York has dropped me as well, I will have to take it,
one bullet at a time, and the first will come from this well-
oiled .544—my hand holds steady the heavy handle while the

wind whips my coat and my ears ring and the fog is burned away and my man says, *Ready*, and that rascal fires first—

His shot flies high, by Theodosia, and I know I'll send him to his long home now—my sole regret that I was born a decade too late to be Father of this State and so will have to win my Fame by might to assure my place in History, to be the man whom everyone recalls by name, and leave as inheritance to my adoring Theodosia—Theodosia, my princess, oh Theodosia— the United States of Burr.

## Dr. David Hosack, 34,
## Noted Physician & Chronicler

In predawn darkness, a knock on my front door pulls me from a dream in which I am staring at myself in the mirror—stark white surgeon's gown and a head enwrapped with thick layers of gauze—my eyes the lone feature—I begin to un-wrap the dressing layer upon layer and it grows pink and red and redder yet, bunching up in the wash basin before me like an aborted foetus—what will my face be beneath, will it even be there—the blood is thick on my hands and tacky as sap and on my gown as well—and now: the blank face behind the lit lamp of the man who beat upon my door and we are off in a skiff across the Hudson, bobbing about, the wind splishing water over my boots, a young boy bailing with a molasses bucket, until we ground ashore beneath the sheer wall of the Palisades, and the world is violently come into focus—two gunshots at dawn and I am already halfway up the path when I spy a man hidden by umbrella scuttling by me like a cat chased from a rubbish bin—am I to feign ignorance the reason I've been summoned; am I not to recognize my friend when he passes four feet from me; am I not to recall that this same stretch of land is where I doctored General Hamilton's son when he lost his life three years before in a duel with pistols; or that this is where I bandaged that Canadian's arm when the Stewart boy cut it during a sword fight last year—Burr too has fought here before, with old Church, from whom he walked away with a mere hole in his topcoat, and he fought another with Senator Jackson, they say, but I'd wager that's apocryphal—still Jackson did kill the lieutenant governor of Georgia, so it is possible—

last year, the editor Coleman killed the New York harbor-master, who was dropped to die on my doorstoop: all this killing in the name of Honor and yet they scurry and hide and lie like rats afterward.

I crest the path, heaving, sleep still crusted in my eye, to see General Hamilton himself—of course it's him—I kneel by his bloody side and see where the bullet has entered and clipped his spine and liver and my lips tremble, *Your Honor, it is mortal*, and his eyes roll back and he mutters, *Death to this disease, Democracy*, and his man says, *You did not hear him, doctor*, and I nod, holding the hand of this man who might have been king in any other country, in any other time, but here is just become one corpse more, and as we carry him to the boat, I recall how Hamilton tirelessly endeavored to undo Burr's career—and now, with the cost of his own life, perhaps he has succeeded at last.

# A Scalping: Thompson v. Asi-yahola

*Outside of Fort King, Big Swamp, Florida,*
*December 28, 1835*

## "General" Wiley Thompson, 53,
## Former Congressman & Current Indian Agent

Nostalgic this morning for my wife's milk gravy thick
with loose sausage slathered in a heap on her fluffy
white biscuits and me in my robe with little else to cover my
modesty—coffee percolating in the fire and bacon popping
in the skillet and she is happy and breaks two eggs to sizzle
in the fat and the sunlight comes through her lace curtains
and she is glowing and humming a tune I do not know,
something from the hymnal I suppose, and this is the life
we always promised one another—soon as the children were
grown and gone, I came home from DC and the madness
of the House—we were both surrounded by babies—but my
pipes stood cold in the pewter tray and the bourbon canter
was empty as she demanded it be so at first chance I cut out
for this detail. *What would you have me do, dear? The heathen ambus-*
*cade the white farmers, snipe them as they try to put order into that wild*
*earth and master it through will and toil and sweat. It is my Christian duty,* I
lied—so I repaired to this land, where even after Christmas it
is boggy as hell, the bugs ambitious about my eyes and ears,
but at least here I can smoke in peace—Erastus keeps his store
chock-full of my cigars, and when Jackson makes me general
for crushing this Osceola and his band of savages, I will keep
a team of islanders to roll them for me at my leisure—and
too my wife got me going to church where, despite my best
raiments, I never felt comfort—here I am sated and sweating
in my wool uniform, the stink of four days' worth of rye rising into my nostrils—my belly full from the cracklin' corn-
bread and venison and beans—yet I hum her tune and think

how good tobacco always tasted right after a good morning romp in the—

A crazed screech splits the air and the scrub brush comes alive with a rush of the ungodly red devils—they are everywhere, like ants, over the ramparts of the fort and into the general store—poor Erastus and all my cigars—I spy Osceola across the field—he stands tall with that rifle Jackson gave me, and I reach for my pistols but only too late: ah, the wasted time, the indecision, the bargains and compromises, and the pains in this life too brief.

## Asi-yahola (a.k.a. Osceola; born Billy Powell), 31, Seminole Warrior

We came to you naked singing the hawk-tail song and offered you the white feather and the black drink and you shackled me, friend, caught me in chains like one of your dark slaves and held me in a cage where I bared my teeth and growled like the wolf until my cunning spirit said to you, *In five days' time I shall bring to you the men of my band*, and you stroked my spine, made a great present of this Spanish rifle whose stock is well oiled and holds the weight of the deer shank, and now I aim it at your head as you waddle from the same fort where you told me what the Great Father demands—you do not know, friend, that on a cool night when the stars crackled in the black sky of my boyhood, the Great Father you serve, General Jackson, led an army of whites and traitorous reds, thick as the summertime locust, to kill and drive us from our homes and we fled into this flat wet country—now that same man threatens that if we do not go to the far side of Mother River to live among the false and faithless Creeks he will send another storm to roll over us—but I will tell every living man this: I am no longer a young blade of grass bending in the big wind, I am now the hard cypress standing strong in swamp water—so bring your thunder and rain, friend, but I will not be swayed and you will not have our land and you will not have our rivers or swamps or sward and you will not have our dignity, which the Breathmaker gives us from his very mouth, and neither will you have our Negroes—not our slaves or Maroons and not my wife and my son, the one you call half-breed, the same as you called me the day you bade me sign the Great

Father's treaty, the one I stabbed with my scalping knife as
my signature as well as my promise: my white half hates you,
friend, and my Muskogee half will make your skull red and
leave it to blacken in the sun while your body is devoured by
the vulture and the rat—

I cry my war whoop and we step into the open and you can
see I am true to my word: I have delivered all of my men—sixty
*hadjo*, each in battle dress singing the death-scalp song and
running straight at you—but do not fear, dear friend, for they
will drive past you and on into the fort—no, I alone will stop
and wait for you to arm yourself before I kill you and share
your scalp with all.

# Bloody Hands, 16 & 54,
## Muskogee Artist & Alleged Witness to the Duel

This controversial piece of ledger art was uncovered by Professor Scott Gage in an antique store outside St. Augustine, Florida. It is a fine specimen; however, its authenticity is disputed and has come under some level of scrutiny. The artist purportedly witnessed this event when he was a teenager and a participant in the Second Seminole War. Some forty years after the event, according to Dr. Gage, Bloody Hands created this art piece while serving in a US government internment camp for Aborigines. Interestingly, he is one of the few ledger artists who are not of Plains Indian origin. In support of the artwork's integrity, Dr. Gage argues that, after the Second Seminole War, many Florida peoples were forcibly relocated to the Oklahoma Territory where, perhaps, Bloody Hands fell in with Sitting Bull and participated in the hit-and-run attacks on US forts in the upper Missouri area during the 1860s. In support of this claim, Dr. Gage points to the fact that Bloody Hands was incarcerated in Fort Yates, where his name appears on various government documents. Later, he was shipped back to Florida and imprisoned in Fort Marion, where he purportedly composed this picture and, later, in 1898, died of pneumonia, accompanied by what doctors at the time described as dementia praecox or, by today's nomenclature, acute schizophrenia.

# Steel Hole by Hole: Henry v. MacKenna

*Laying Train Tracks through the West Virginia Mountains,
September 27, 1871*

# John Henry, 28,
## Steel-Driving Man

Done drove twenty durn miles of line and that machine on my heels steady behind, comin down on me like rain on the tin roof above where I slept as a youngun—chicken and dumplins stewin in the pot lure me out a dream of Daddy comin home from the workhouse with a sackful of orange rock candy, back into the world of Ma Ma Ma and she be hammerin home her orders with that two-inch-thick belt she call "Mercy"—*Get yo ass out that bed and slop them hogs, boy, and gather them greens fore I tan yo hide*—I shore do as she say and when I come back it's her ladlin in our best bowl the chicken and ramps and carrots and pellets of dough—I come over the top again for the ten one thousandth time today and my bones brittle beneath my muscles all stove up and tight—a pang of fire runs right through my arm and catches a stitch in my heart—I hear a poundin there and know that machine gonna pound on past, poundin, like Ms. Freeman poundin on the front door, her askin Ma if she's seen the egg layers that skidaddled out her yard, and if we find em, wouldn't we please just please let her know and I get the guilt-face lookin at the food afore me but Ma just suck her teeth and say, *Nah, Miss Lady, I ain't see no bird 'round here today*—I like to of died from shame but Ma say Miss Lady a uppity-actin old biddy anyway, say she just wish I'd drop dead of a stroke fore she'd even give one yard bird back to that uppity-actin old biddy—I remember a dozen times when I squeamed at loppin the head off a hen but Ma would grab that heavy axe out my hand quick as you please and say, *What kindly man you gon be?* And she'd cut that thing clean in two and hand me back that tool and say, *Don't never you need to send no man to do what a woman can damn well do, because she will, by God, and do it even better too.*

I am my mother's stout arms steady swingin my axe down on chicken necks and it clangs and sparks and trues the rail and I slip to a knee and my hammer fails and I grab up my arm, it burnin like the stew on the stove top, burnin, and I can't hardly breathe—breathless, headless—I fall on my side and see Ma Ma Ma in the mountaintop cawin like crows shakin they tail feathers, she shakin her head, sayin, *Who is the chicken now, my big baby boy?*

## Conor MacKenna, 57,
## Protestant & Foreman of the L & N Train Line

I willna lose this contest, not to him nor any of his kind,
what lost me both me boys, Owen and Callum, in the
war conscripted by Lincoln, leaving me alone with the great
herd of hogs and slop and row upon row of wheat and corn
and oats and the rye I'd fashion into a fine little whisky—I
was forced to sell our Pennsylvania farm—both me boys killed
wandering in the Virginia, cold and hungry, fighting for the
freedom of these blasted brutes and for what, so this black
blow-in could destroy me livelihood now by unionizing me
labor, well by God, industry will win ever time, boyo, and
these men can become memory a-fadin just like that Yokum
boy what jumped me back when I was but a lad and I come
home with the torn collar and the bloody nose and upset me
mam, saying through me tears, *That Lamar Yokum and his two big
brothers ganged up on me and salted me somehow fierce,* now thinking I'd
get me a coddle, but me mam caught me up by me eartop and
marched me down to their shack and shouted their ma to the
front porch and called her all kinds of nasty names—bitches
and cunts and such—said, *Look here at what your little monkeys have
done,* and me lip throbbed great against each pounding pulse
and I smiled as their ma beat em about the heads with the ladle
she held and the boys begged and scurried and Lamar swore
he'd done the deed his lone self and so me mam said, *Well, I
don't believe that for one feckin second now, do I?* and me tongue swoll in
me mouth, liked to of choked me dead, it did, and we tumbled
and we tussled and he busted me lip once more and he busted
me nose this time too and I slipped in the slick grass and he

pinned me arms down with his knees and I could smell that
sour pig smell on him and then he just vanished—heroically,
me mam had snatched him from off me but then she began
to beat me gob with the ham of her fists, yelling, *I'll teach you to
lie to me, you rotten bastard, you!* and for what all I know she was
right—I have never even laid eyes upon me father—I cockroached
out from under her and lost me shoes and still I ran all the way
home in me sock feet, which got all soaked and one slipped
halfway off and flopped and flapped about me, but she caught
me up and she beat me arse-end with a thin switch for a good
long while and to this day I still have the scars to show for it—

And then this here bluegum he falls and I know he's not
to prove whatever he thinks he was set to prove and his union
will be busted, me machines are the future of labor, aye, and
sure now I can visit me mam's grave and tell her, *You were right all
along, dear—can't no coon whip me, Ma.*

## Seamus O'Reily, 54,
### Catholic & Union Representative for the Railway Employees' Department of the AFL, June 18, 1922

Sure now, I seen him do it, lads, and with me own two blasted eyes when I was but a baby boy—he beat that engine and then he beat that fat cat West Brit too, just as they're doing back in the old country now, aye, and he stood tall as any two of yous and his chest was big around as a Jameson barrel and he had two hammers for fists and a black hound what would follow him 'round both day and night but was nowheres to be found on that day yer man Henry left us—I was but a boy, as I've said, but, by Jeanie Mac, he was swinging those fists so furious that a whirl of wind whipped up and spun from the ground and the earth shook and the sweat rained off him like yer cow pissin on a flat rock but then that rainbow bloomed above his broad shoulders and haloed his head as he beat that machine, which moaned and wheezed about—and when yer man cried out for his dear ma-ma, I swear to the Virgin Herself, that engine whined *ma-ma* as well—but afore he left us, Mr Henry hisself reached over and took that hard-driving boss man Protestant piece of shit what he was, the kind who scuttles about doing the bidding of the Big Boss—the same man who'd stake claims to half yer wages but keep ya blistered in the sun all day a-dyin—Mr Henry took that same bastard by his ankles, turned him half over and up'ards and drove him as a spike right clean through the line and the skies parted and Mr Henry rose through the clouds, unbeaten even by death, and I seen it I swear with me own two eyes—Mr Henry, he was a deadly sharp man, much more than any single man among us, but if we all band together, brothers, band as one, we could walk off this job and picket this Wheeling Way Line, and even with their strike busters and their Pinkertons, we could shut her down the same as Mr Henry shut down that damn machine and we can hold out till we get what's right and ours, aye—so I stand afore you now, lads, one machinist among many, so you may see with your own two eyes, me, the man you've elected to represent ya, use my very own voice, like Mr Henry's hammers, to bring down the call for a strike!

# Into the Greasy Grass: Custer v. Ska

*During the Battle of Little Big Horn on the Crow Reservation,*
*the Montana Territory,*
*June 25, 1876*

## George Armstrong Custer, 36,
## Lieutenant Colonel of the US Seventh Cavalry

As I drive Victory through the river and urge my men
to follow, a whole horde of the heathen rise from the
brush of the banks and train their rifles and arrows on us,
so I fire my carbine till the barrel tip glows red and my cheek
burns and my ear becomes a ringing hollowed bell—one shot
hits my trunk and carries me off my mount, and when I hit
the water, my breath quits me and all I can see is the face of
Grant—his general stars taken out and polished by his black
manservant; his swollen fingers wrapped 'round the stem of
the champagne flute he hoists, muttering a toast to our nation's
centennial; his yellowed eyes steadfast upon the bottle—I rise
from the water, rivulets streaming behind my ears, my twin
English Bulldog pistols barking in my hands—I unleash hand-
fuls of shot and I am enshrouded in hot white smoke, thick as
the bouquet of Queen Anne's lace I gave Libbie on our wedding day—I should be the one standing before the assembled
Congress, entreating our Lord to protect our nation, my adoring Libbie by my side, silk spilling over her bustle, as an artist
makes our portrait for the White House walls—Grant sent me
here because of the kickback scandal and to avenge his foolish
brother Orville and Secretary Belknap for the truths I spoke of
them before Congress, but I always did look good in the press,
so I acquiesced, *It shall be my honor, Mr. President, to serve at your behest
and clear the way for peace and progress*, but you, sir, shall know my
cavalier genius and pin all four stars to my blue coat, the one
Libbie will clean and press with her own hands—now the guns'
ivory handles lie cool against my skin and before me stands my

assassin, the man I have missed with each damn shot—he levels his rifle and all I have left is this one prayer: perhaps a single bullet lies hidden in the guts of these guns. So heave-chested and steely-eyed as the morning sun, I aim my sidearms and charge, high-stepping through the water, the wind cooling my skin as I squeeze the triggers on these empty chambers, squeeze them as gentle as if they were Libbie's pale hands.

His last bullet, Lord, has found its mark and passes through every folding drape of my brain and I fall back again and see the sky one final time before the cold water clouds my eyes but it does not hurt, Libbie, I swear, not a bit compared to never having you sew epaulettes square on my shoulders again.

## Ptebloka Ska (a.k.a. White Cow Bull), 28, Oglala Sioux Warrior

I had soaped myself in bull lard against the cool waters of the Greasy Grass, where I swam this morning ahead of battle with the bluecoats, and I was lying naked to the loincloth in yucca and sage grasses when like the hawk they bushwhacked us—crossed the coulee upstream unannounced and raided our camp—I crawl behind the rocks where I had stood my weapons, wanting only the head of their leader, Long Locks, who years ago kidnapped fair Mo-nah-se-tah and forced his baby inside her and though I have spoken to her only through the open flaps of her teepee, I love her and have wished in my best heart to walk with her under a courting blanket and make her my wife, but she has rejected me because I said I would even welcome her bastard blond boy, the one they say twins Long Locks's likeness, so last night I sang the suicide song and I danced till the drums and my heart were one and I came out here to war with no belief I would ever return alive to my tribe, and since I cannot find the man I want, that coward and rapist, I will, in his stead, have the head of another, so I blast from his saddle the first pink man who rides through the cottonwood trees and the water weighs down the buckskin clothes he wears to hide his hairy body but he rises from the river like Great Medicine itself, his voice growling like a wolf as it eats— one brave white man at last—I freeze and let him fire his bullets but they will not have me—they fly by whistling like notes played through an eagle-bone flute—and so he charges and I put my next shot straight through his skull and shrill and take my hatchet for a coup, hoping some Sioux will later tell Mo-nah-se-tah of my courage.

Like a lover, his half-Sioux traitor collects him in his arms and I drop my rifle and I catch by its mane the dead man's pinto and spring to its back and heft my hatchet high and holler the war cry Crazy Horse has taught us to live by: *Hoka hey*, I shout, *hoka hey: it is a good day to die, but an even better day to kill.*

## Mitch Bouyer, 39,
## Custer's Chief of Scouts, Half French & Half Sioux

When Custer went down, I hopped from my rack-
of-bones pony and ran in after him, my heart tight
as a fist in my throat, yet fore I could reach him he rose and
charged into the hornets' nest and still I followed and the warrior stood awfully still with clumps of earth and prairie grass
clinging to his skin like Wakantanka's own revenge—bullets
and dogs are everywhere and Custer's head explodes against
my face, a chip of bone blinding my right eye, and I catch his
falling corpse and some bastard calls to me, *Let him go, you goddamn half-breed*, and kicks me loose and takes him away—the earth
under the water trembles as the braves thunder by on horseback, routing the whites who scatter like blackbirds, and I am
kneeling half blind in the water when a chill-shadow covers
me, a silhouette horse rearing, its stockinged hooves thrashing, and I make out its belly and chest and neck and giant
head, and I know I should not be here and I know I should
not have befriended Custer. I should not have translated the
Blue Coat treaties, which I knew to be lies and, because they
came from my lips, became my lies too. I should have stayed
with Magpie as she suckled our newborn and I should have
chased our children about the teepee, laughing, and I should
have roasted them rabbits on spits as the moon crested the
hills and the ponies whinnied in the distance. I should have
made clear to Custer that Sioux and buffalo are not two but
one and that slaughter of the animal is slaughter of the man.
I should have killed Custer in his sleep. I should have braided
my horse's mane with feathers and colored twine, put my blue

clay handprint on its haunch and ridden alongside this warrior here who now sets his pinto down, the man rising in sight
like something come over the horizon, yet he remains only a
shadow, a shade, with his hatchet held high.

I put my arms across my bloody face as if to block a.bril-
liant light but then drop them by my sides and rise to my
feet and raise my chin and say in my purest Lakota, *Go ahead,
tanhanši, and try to cleave me in two any more than I already am.*

# Fiesta de Semana Santa:
# Fuego v. Lopez y Avaloz

*During the Fifth* Corrida de Toros *of Easter Sunday*
*in Granada, Spain,*
*March 27, 1932*

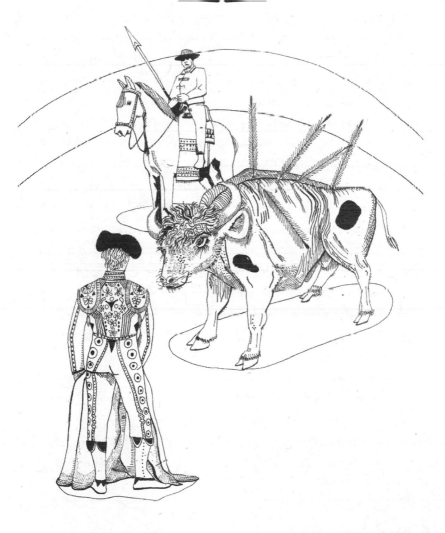

## Sueño de Fuego, 5, 584 Kilos, Miura Bull from La Ganadería Miura Lineage

Scratch and snort and huff and puff and put my hoof-print in this earth—this my place and this my time and here I've come to fuck or fight—here I find no cow nor steer to my delight, so stomp and spit and huff and thrust and put my rut in this beast here—six legs, it has, three arms, two heads—has it come to muscle me, to make a morsel out of me—but truth be told, I want it more, so I drive my horn straight through its torso, and even as it barbs my hide, I lift it from the earth, shift my hump and dump it rump-wise and tear its insides out—I stomp and bellow, grumble and dig and suffer as it dies.

Jabbed and hooked four men today and drove them each and all away—they barbed and barbed but I drove them each away—now comes their god, skin of shiny lights, who cries and spins and shouts and hides behind a bright red cape that goes a swishy sway, and it ripples like heifer scruff when I mount and huff and puff and grunt my calf-make rut—I rush and rush but it twirls and I spin and crash and fall again until the red is me running from my snoring snout and coming in strings from my open mouth—still the cape goes wiggle waggle more—I rake my hoof and miss my mark and grunt and puff and thrust my horn twice more into earth, holes each the size of this god's waist—about me roars the horde who wave their small white rags and shriek for ears and tail and more—*Toro*, he cries and *Toro*, again—and my wind blows out the holes in me and so too goes my blood—I cannot lift my head, I am bone-rattled and beaten, defeated in battle—and now my nape lies smooth, my tense muscles unknot—I'll soon be leaving this body behind, rise over the moon to the Great Pasture beyond, in time to join my harem of grazing long-lashed gals who will swoon and low when they gaze at me and raise their swishy tails.

*Toro*, he calls again, and though my mouth is slick with blood, I will not show my tongue nor shake the sticks stuck near my spine; no, let them whistle till their lips go numb but I will bristle at dirt no more nor snort nor snore nor warn nor bluff, but wait till time is mine and true and ripe with proof, and then, horns low, I will charge.

## Ignacio Lopez y Avaloz, 31, 64 Kilos,
## Famed Matador from Priego de Córdoba

I urge the bull to meet my half-cocked thrust and bravely
die same as he fought but now he balks and so we stare
like the last two lovers alive, each facing death without the
other: Oh Lord, bring this noble beast to rest before my feet
and tonight I will spread Your word to the heathen women
of Granada, passing my tongue through their plump lips as
if they were plucked rose petals pressed between the pages of
Your book. *Toro, toro,* I call yet he does not move, though I have
twisted him in pass upon pass, spinning blood from his hump
to freckle the ochre earth, packed hard as my cock I sacrifice to
virgins who come nightly to cool my nerves, which thrum as
did the organs of La Catedral de Santa María when I was but a
babe and wiry and ill-behaved, wriggling in Mama's lap, and
the music bellowed through the open mouths of pipes as large
as lances and I would shriek, a sound lost among the din, and
she would rub my face with the soft skin of her hands yet deny
me suckle again and again and I'd cry the more demanding
milk, my earnest hunger never filled. I set my jaw and stamp my
foot and holler yet again, *Toro!*

The drums roll and the horns swell and the bull comes
and I cross before him, sword straight out, but he swings his
head at me, unbinds me from the earth, and my mouth goes
dry as silenced organ pipes and the world becomes a singular
hiss, as when Mary's milk missed the saint's lips and scalded
on a searing stone, and I smack against the ground and the air
explodes from my lungs and back and a fire burns riot through
my guts while I try to suck and suck and suck—

# Jose "Pepe" Hernandez, 33, 61 Kilos, Ferdinand's *Mozo de Espadas* from Valencia

Ignacio poses before his bull like Saint George above his dragon and he lays the Toledo steel estoque across the blood-red muleta, which the wind catches and flaps about, exposing his thighs—I should have soaked the flannel cape, put more weight on its hem against the whipping of this weird wind but now I'm lost in his paso doble: the man and his cape and the bull in his cape form an ephemeral statue that spins painfully slow and tight, the blood of the bull brushes a streak across the gold-threaded buttons, which I fastened for Ignacio not two hours ago when I'd sewn him into his pants and plaited his hair, pinning it beneath his felt montera—as I knelt before him buffing his shoes, I looked up and caught the pity in his eyes, as if he and I had not once competed for top purses until I was gored by a bull, leaving me instead a cripple who will never fight another bull nor carry the full Fiesta de Semana Santa bier again—the bull charges Ignacio and as one mouth the arena gasps and I am a child in the old caves at the beach, where the waves broke against the vaulted rocks, the water receding and sucking the air out with it, tugging the breath from my young lungs, and I stood shocked-still and numb until the next wave came with cold spray and brought my senses back—the bull has buried his horn hilt-deep in the belly of Ignacio and he is as dead as this bull soon will be, his body dragged by horse and rope from *plaza* to *matadero* where his head will be removed, hide stripped, meat butchered, shipped to market, and sold to people still mourning the loss of Ignacio, who will have his own body hoisted onto the shoulders of toreadors who will bear him to Catedral de la Encarnación, where he will lie in repose five days and nights lit dimly by candle for pilgrims come the world over to kneel by the hundreds and thousands and smear their tears and fingerprints across his glass coffin, covering it with roses and rosaries, and wail as he's carried to the Cuevas de Sacromonte and buried there in full regalia—people will speak of him in cafes, will read of him every Easter in newspapers, will name their children after him, and some will even come to worship him as we both did Romero.

But I will simply sew a black brassard about my right sleeve and limp on to a new torero, whom I will dress and assist and hold his estoque and muleta, which I will wet so that it hangs heavy enough to hide him from the eyes of the bull.

# Night of the Chicken Run:
## Summers v. Scarborough

*Dueling Cars on a Dirt Road between Fields of Garlic,*
*Gilroy, California,*
*June 2, 1967*

## Charles "Chaz" Summers, 18,
## Driving His Father's 1965 Thunderbird

**B**ad enough Sara had to neck on this greaser with a duck-
butt haircut from another time but did she have to do
it behind the gym while wearing my letterman jacket—that's
what her girlfriends told me and that's what drove me mad—
I couldn't just bust his face with fists, that would be like hitting
him on the football field, where I ruled as middle linebacker
knocking hell out of crossing receivers, catching their ribs
and stealing their breath, until we played the Fresno Warriors
and that cheap shot garbled my knee to goo, and so went the
season and my scholarship, too, though Sara's still leaving
this fall—in spite of my Brooks Brothers chinos and bleeding
madras shirts, despite that my old man owns these fields and the
largest mill in town—my folks won't come off with that kind of
cash, no matter how good a school Stanford is—so this field
will be my life and each summer I will wait for the garlic leaves
to brown and die and then I will harvest and store the bulbs as
well—surely this is the place where I will die or over in the mill,
boxing stinking roses for someone else to eat—yet even after the
surgery, when I'd see her in my jacket, my pride would swell,
the way her hair fell straight over the big blue *G*—she's leaving next week, rubbing it in my face with this hood rat here—I
know I shouldn't have slapped her at the pre-grad bash but
I was cranked up and drunk and she was going on about the
scene and saying, *Dig it, man*, like Maynard G. Krebs, high on
grass—the politics and the music and the war and all that—I
could have let it all pass except tonight I saw them in the back of
his car, dry-humping to that hippie-dip music—it was my dad

who taught me how to truly hurt a man—crush his body or take his pride—so I called the dirt leg out to this dim lane to put his nerve and ride on the line—now I'm in my dad's T-bird with power everything to show Sara one last time that I'm her man and that this could still be our summer of love.

Bouncing in the light of his one good beam, rushing to meet him head-on as in some anxious dream in which there's no waking nor escape, I'm lost in a fog thick as pigskin and I can't find Sara. *Sara!* I scream, *Sara!* and I veer left at the last second and hit the ditch and the coil springs collapse and flex and I am airborne, weightless as a ball tossed across the middle of a football field.

## George Scarborough, 19,
## Driving a Rebuilt 1947 Packard Clipper Deluxe

Damn my muddy shoes and my greasy nails and damn this day and this night as well and all this useless mean pride—this fathead flattop prep too dense to let Sara go and me too hardheaded to say no even to this stupid challenge here—damn Kerouac and his kicks and Brando and Dean's too—*What is a man to do, Daddy?*—these stained jeans and this untucked tee and these rolled cigs in my sleeve and this one in my lips and the two I hot-boxed before—my mouth's a damn dry wad of dirty rags—I slick my hides into the earth and mash the gas and jam the box into gear, my hands quaking over the leather, and I hear the loose earth crunching under tires as I tear ass down this lane, my back slammed into the bucket by the accelerator I built myself, but man, if I had a shot of rye for every time Pops told me I was garbage to be left curb-side, I'd have drowned by now and been done with this wretched race and this damn road, this bumpy rough way, the stinking sweet bulbs that chalk up my throat and close my nose till I can barely even breathe—damn my old man for ever bringing me to this podunk hick shit town and damn this engine we bored out together, the only useful thing he ever taught me to do, and damn Pops's popskull whisky breath and beard scruff across my neck, and for the times I'd drop a wrench, double-damn them cherry cigs he'd burn into my collarbone—damn my mom for leaving him but not taking me along—and damn this souped-up car and these bent eight pistons and 380 stroker I rebuilt myself, and damn this shove-shifter and the damn power of this damn engine rattling through the steering wheel and into my wrists, my damn thin wrists, my damn hand heels gone numb as I race her again like I once did Sara.

And damn you too, girl—I know you were using me—it's clear as his headlights growing larger by the second; saw you sidle up to your old pals, smiling in the gravel lot—you were slumming, Sara, but goddamn it, did you have to damn me too: here on this single-lane dirt road built for tractors and big truck traffic, searing between two fields of ripe garlic, I know you'll go back with him but I'll be damned first before you ever do—I see him flinch and swerve left and I rev my engine for one last chance at revenge and I swing myself right, right into him.

# The 1967 Class of the Gilroy High Mustangs, Witnesses to the Game of Chicken

Like we knew something was wrong when Sara first showed up to homeroom with a black eye, telling lies about running into locker doors, and later when she and Chaz broke up, like officially, and she stopped wearing his class ring on her choker chain—like we knew there'd be all kinds of drama and stuff when next week she came to class with an open collar and three brazen hickeys bruised across her neck like constellations—we knew tonight would end badly when Jo Anne and Todd told Chaz they'd seen Sara parked in that greaser's car at the Tastee Licks Cream and Burgers— when we found them later at the drive-in, like we knew if they fistfought we'd all jump in because greasers have no second thoughts about knives or brass knuckles or fair fights of any kind but we never saw this coming.

It was all Chaz's idea but who could have imagined the collision would be so great—both cars burning down the lane while we jumped and jeered and egged Chaz on until they swerved toward each other and hit that furrow and left the ground—they like hung there in a cool picture for a full second that felt like eternity—then Chaz's car sort of split in two and exploded and raced in shrapnel and flame through the garlic field and we ran to the crash but the greaser's car blew up too and like we knew they both were dead and all and the fire got so big and high we lost sight of the stars and the fire followed the gas that ran deep through the runnels and that sweet stench seared our nostrils like when your mom tries to make roasted garlic but burns it and the whole house stinks for

weeks—the smoke was everywhere like the tule fog that winter
we tried to make the band-camp battle in Alameda but got
stuck on the 101 in that twenty-car pileup and Jason and Todd
got in a shove fight on the bus—it was like that but way way
worse—and we knew that later we'd have to explain this wreck
to our parents and the police and it would be in the papers
from Sacramento to Santa Barbara and we knew what had happened, that they had both killed themselves, and we all agreed
that we needed to agree and we all agreed that what we needed to
say was, *It was all that greaser's fault; he killed our best friend.*

# Dueling Banjos in the Key of A: Redden v. Cox

*On the Set of* Deliverance, *Clayton, Georgia,*
*May 10, 1971*

## "Lonnie (Banjo Boy)," 16, as Played by Billy Redden

They've come to worship the river god but he is wrath-
ful and his minions are legion and they demand
sacrifice—because I like his glasses, his ring, his smile, I want
to warn him away from death downstream but I have no sound
but what comes from my fingertips and thumb—my muscles
taut against the strings, strumming and pecking a warning he
may not cipher—now he's following me, strum peck, strum
peck, note after note and we're slow-slithering down the
mouth of these sounds to a place I want him to see but I want
to go faster like snakes swimming with the pull of water coming fast on me in the river, bitten, and I hollered, *Mommy*,
the last word I'd ever speak and my fever burned out my skin
and eyes, my swollen tongue filled the whole of my mouth but
now I want to go faster and faster and he's keeping up where
I lead him down the river to warn him—faster past snakes'
slitheriness into faster-pulling water, dangerfast—I go strum
peck strum peck like the constant ticktock of time measured out
one tick at a tock time, by river god, and time thrums through
the bones of the world—rocks and trees, birds on wings, the
scurry of small things in the night, the slithering of snakes
and rivers and snakes in rivers, slithering—the river god's
voice also slithers along the snake's spine—the bumpy rocks in
the white water babbling is also the voice of the river god thrum-
ming, drawing my fingers to his mouth to grab his tongue same
as that snake took hold of mine and we will grab hold when
we die and enter that great maw forever and we'll crawl inside
like a venom waiting to be spat out in his songs, hallelujah,

and summon the others to follow, lure them in for a song, but I must warn this man because he is not ready to sing, he cannot keep up, and this life goes so fast fast fast and the snake's fangs pierced my tongue, put its venom there and locked my jaw shut, but my hands are free to yell strumpeck strumpeck strumpeck but then he stops.

## "Drew Ballinger" 32,
## as Played by Ronny Cox

Everyone here's missing something—fingers, teeth, half
their minds—take this kid, to look at him with his wide
eyes and a face bland as a boiled egg you'd never know he is a
great banjo picker, a real live hillbilly savant, like you'd only see
in movies, and he wants to play with me and I keep thinking
what I heard my brother, the professor, once say, *Music is time
meted out like the pendulum of a grandfather clock measuring our lives one note
at a time*, and that's true, I guess, like water steadily sliding away,
under a bridge, and gone. In the key of A: G, C, G. *Come on,
I'm with you*—maybe he's not so special, maybe I'm just naïve—
I can't trust my judgment on these things like when we were
in Helena, Arkansas, and I saw this old black man banging
spoons against his thighs, his tip hat set out before him, and
I shrugged and my brother turned me around, told me how
special and antique this style of percussion was—something
about the Civil War and drum and fife music. I nail this kid's
eighth and quarter notes, I know that much, but I wish my
brother were here now; he went to school to learn to appreci-
ate this kind of thing. Bet he could tell me about the ethno-
graphic importance of this music to this culture—tell me
about the history of call and response, the influence of the
Scots Irish folk traditions, and its significance in a greater
anthropological context—I just want someone to confirm
that this kid's the real deal, that he's a living relic, and that
I'm truly living in the moment and that this is a rare, special
time—he picks that banjo so quick I can't keep up and sweat is
beading on my forehead and lip and there's a fly buzzing in my

ear but I can't move my hand to shoo it—this feels so authentic, but how can I tell? I can't even remember what it's like to be authentic anymore—everything in life feels prescriptive, like a rehearsal of something I've already seen on TV—my brother used to tell me all about it but I never listened enough, never listened to anyone enough, and that's why I'm here with Lewis, with this boy, with this music, and I'm so tired of all this self-doubt—it's like I can't ever get out of my own head, like now, Drew, you're doing it again and suddenly I'm lost and I say, *I'm lost*, and the music stops, drowned by my overthinking, and I'm left alone with a silence that fills the gap between my fear and insecurity and I say, *Goddamn, you play a mean banjo*, and I hold out my hand but he turns away and that's it—I'm going to experience something real even if it kills me.

# Burt Reynolds, 35,
## Playing "Lewis Medlock"

How many takes they gon' use of these two playing guitars—
hell the inbred ain't even frettin' his own banjo—why
am I even here today—I know it's the first day but I'm hardly in
these shots and I am the gotdamn star of this picture—I know
these guys are all professionals—Jon fresh off that Academy
gigolo picture and Ronny and Ned from Broadway—but damn,
I wouldn't have played Ned's role for all the Oscars in the pig-
squealing world—I am glad Dickey's gone, bad enough he'll be
back with all his loud talk and bragging ways to play the sheriff—
I'm the man with the muscles and sweat the ladies want to see,
so what if I wear lifts and a toupee, it's all for art, and there's two
little homegrown peaches waiting in my trailer right now who
I'd like to bite on their fuzzy navels but I need to stay focused,
rub my triceps I just swelled with push-ups and dips—focus,
man, and prove everyone wrong who said I only got this gig
'cause I made Carson laugh, like I'm just some pretty boy
jock with no talent beyond my smile—Daddy likes old Johnny
but when I asked if he'd seen me on *The Tonight Show*, he said,
*I ain't watch it last night,* and I said, *Daddy, I was on there every night last
week,* and he shrugged like he always shrugs, the stoic lawman—
but Burt, baby, just breathe and scowl because Boorman needs
you to lead these three goobers, the serious cat out here in the
coon-on-a-log country—I think again of Daddy and his hard-
nosed Cherokee scowl that I imitate, cock my head like him
until I feel like my father, the sheriff who fills up doorways and
made me feel like a small muck-about all my life until I called
him last month and said, *Daddy, you were right all along: I am a quitter.*

*I quit football, I quit college, I quit my work, and now I've quit my marriage too*, and he said, *Come on home, son, and I'll tell you all the things I've quit in my life*, and in that moment, it was like he'd said, *Once you recognize what a fuckup you are, then you are on your way to being a man*, and man, you ain't no man until your daddy says you are.

And Boorman calls *cut* and comes over and drapes his arm over my shoulder and says, *Burt, baby, you were perfect, you're going to carry this picture*, and I just scowl and nod like the man I am.

# Peleas de Gallo: Caesar v. I Am

*In the Last Legal Cockfight in the United States,*
*Pumpkin Center, Louisiana,*
*August 15, 2008*

## Caesar Julius, 29 Months,
## Dan Gray Roundhead, 4.02 lbs, Record: 8–0

A peace stills the certain center of me when he takes my beak inside his mouth, rubs my fluff feathers, and settles the jerking muscles along my spine—he does not call me chanticleer nor the vile cock but rather *Caesar*, always *Caesar*, cooing with his sweet hands on me—even as they dubbed my wattle and comb, his look calmed me—his eyes focus my attention, save me from all distraction: the pickups eaten by rust and rent with neglect; the old man pushing the wheelbarrow filled with ice water and cans of beer, shouting above the other shouts of men with cash and knives pushed at each other; the smells of turpentine and sawdust, whiskey and tobacco—so I'll crow from the mountaintops: I love my man more than my hens—shameful to some, I know, like this rooster strutting across from me, contempt nested there in his eyes, yet in these last still moments before combat I can't help myself: I slip into thoughts of his hands on my back cape, stroking my neck, and the solemn way he takes the leather straps and wets them and fastens the razor-gaffs to my spur stumps and runs his thumbnails up the ridges of my shank—sometimes I feign fevered exhaustion just so he'll spit in my mouth, almost, but never quite, quenching my thirst—for his affections I have become lethal, killing again and again, and though I hate the spurting gore I cause, my fellow birds bleeding their lives out for me, I'd bathe gladly preening in their guts for the joy it brings my man—

And this puffed-up Bantam across from me will be no different: steady me, Sun, and forgive me please my unnatural love, but I will have my man crow once more, *Caesar! Caesar!*

# I Am, 26 Months,
## O'Neal Red, 4.07 lbs, Record: 6–0

Me rooster strut daddy, me señor cock of the walk,
gotta prick longer than yo' talon gaff—look at this
maricón, this capon they've brought me to slay, too lazy to
learn his proper pecking order place—I put him just above
these sad-ass men who've come to see the rooster snuft again
but ain't brought enough fire to kill me yet—I can see it in
his eyes, his cooing eyes cooing that cock handler's eyes—but
what's a man to me but a builder of fences and cages, while
I am free with skill enough to holler the Sun, and the Sun
know better than not rise when I peck and call. Because I Am
the greatest—been blessed with this chest, swollen and strong
as any Bantam you ever saw—when asked why fight, I say, *Why
not?*—I Am: hot like July sand, like God don't give a damn,
and it ain't nothing but a thang for me to survey my land
perched ten feet off the ground, while empty-headed chicken
heads empty they eggs into my nests—I Am: still here because
I say you ain't, and because I say it, boy, you ain't—I Am:
bowed up and just so purty, watch how I dance my cockerel-
waltz—and when you call me *fighter*, I correct, and say *killer*:
four pounds of fury ready for any round robin, rounding up
robins and bobbin jays straying too close to the lane, keepin
them fox and snake at bay.

And you, you needs to pray, Little One, for the odd
chance to find any one of my tail feathers fallen, use it as a
talisman to conjure the devil, and when you do, ask him for
me: *Which came first, Old Scratch, the chicken or the egg?* And that old-
timer will tell you every time, *That badass bird, I Am!* I Am.

## Hector Velazquez, 32,
## Caesar Julius's Cocker

We release the birds and they high-step and prance—
through the slash of gaffs, which strobe the lights, I
see a police who looks so much like the man who took Miguel
away after he knifed that *jefe* in the Ponchatoula strawberry
patch, that no-paying liar who made slaves of us both—stabbed
him as Caesar now stabs his foe, the bird falling and turning
away, so we handlers rush into the *gallodrome* to separate them
and the other cocker slips Caesar's blade out his bird's heart,
which bursts in throbs, his life only worth the making of small
puddles in the sawdust, and the policeman is in the ring now
holding us together, his stick in my back—tomorrow if we
bring our cocks to fight, a thing which is true to their own fowl
nature, he will arrest us, send me home to Guadalajara or to
his pen where my brother spent his last years having to stick
and stab to stay alive, a pen like Caesar has never known—he
strikes my wrist and I drop Caesar and the other bird falls on
him, jabs his gaff into Caesar's neck, the two joined now forever in death, and a metallic clanging erupts on the bleachers,
these men with money to win and lose press in on me—these
cracker and coonass and cowboy alike—crowd against me to
see which dead bird has become dead bird first and they holler threats and bargains and I am outnumbered as always, their
hands and heat upon me, the smell of diesel from the genera-
tors makes me woozy, sweat drips off my nose and I look up,
fresh air and strings of gay lights sway in the rafters, and shouts
rise like the hair on my neck, and I look down at his bird,
whose eyes have gone from glass to gravy—Caesar has won,

but how much longer will he live, his eyes a dying fire burning into mine and I lift him to me and whisper, *Caesar, Caesar*, and I stroke his neck and turn to leave but the police pushes his stick in my belly, just as they stuck their stick in my brother's arm, sending him to his final home rest, and I double over mad as a wet hen, and when that cop says, "Where you think you're going, boy," I reach one hand into my *penche* pants pocket to be cooled by the steel of my switchblade and pray for the courage of my brother and Caesar, to strike as *mi hermano* and *mi hermanito* both did: to stab and stick, to kill and die.

# PART II: † CHALLENGE

# A Saint and His Dragon: George v. Dragon

*Outside of Silene, Libya,*
*299 AD*

# George, 23,
## Soldier, Christian, & Future Saint

Nine days I've ridden without so much as a handful
of palm dates or a palmful of almonds or a bellyful of
goat's milk, when I come over the tumescent hills, swollen and
rolling out to sea, to be made witness to this ancient tableau:
a young girl in billowing silk skirts fastened by her wrists to the
twisted branches of a thick olive tree; behind her a dragon, dry
brown scales dull in this dim light, smoke in curlicues rising
from its snout and open mouth. My manroot rises and strains
against this armor—God has summoned me to this mission,
I have no doubt, to save this lady's flesh from the foul unholy
beast and to spread His holy word to the people of this land,
stunned ignorant by the pagan laws of Rome, and I know this
urge in my loins is yet another challenge the Lord's laid before
me, another desire to drive mortal man mad—how easy a task
must that be?—as a child in Palestine I'd grind myself into
turtle shells or frog mouths or doughy mounds of barley and
exhaust myself there until Father, disgusted and distraught,
sold me to the Roman army and I became a soldier designed
for slaughter until the One True God showed me the light and
grace of Jesus and His body in my mouth and His blood on my
tongue—still these temptations swell and rise and burst about
me and even so I advance, the wind and blood roaring in my
ears like Satan's locusts come to deafen me, yet I advance all
the more swiftly, charge straight into its eyes, black and cold
and empty—its forked tongue flickers venomous and its wings
spread wide and it spits flames that char my shield, which does
not betray me, and still I come forward and slam my lance,

which shatters against this creep's deep breast, and I'm thrown from my mount.

Once as a new soldier in Diocletian's cavalry, I became so frail that I fell from my mount and landed in a pile of barley hay and the smell overcame me—the fields of my youth, where I copulated with earthen bowls of grain and the still-warm side of a sacrificed lamb—here again I find myself aroused and the ache of my manhood plows facedown in the earth, the wind blows under my steel skin, and I rush at the dragon, which rears on its hind legs, and I drive my sword hilt-deep into its lovely groin and I release again and flee: *Oh Lord, look upon me not with scorn but with pity and call my name once more to ring among the hallowed halls of Heaven.*

# The Dragon, the Age of Man

By day I hide within the caves of Tripoli and I sleep in their shadows and folds, by night I fly through the sky or crawl over the land or swim far upon the water, and I am your greatest fears, human—you cannot reason with me or come to terms with me or soothe or coerce or mitigate me, not with all the rubies in the Turk's great vault nor all the flesh of your doughy young virgins nor your roaming goats nor your shaky faith—to appease me you slaughter your own, kill one another to advance your claim over land and sea, or you bring me a wee child and chain her to the rocky outcrops and beg me take her, only her—and I will eat, human, because I must—I am the guardian of the sacred fire so the flames from my mouth are sacrificial, the same as the heat from your own bodies, which burn the sacrifice you take through your mouths—all things that live must die and be consumed, so the whole world is a fire even at its very core and that is what haunts you most—that is what you cannot bring yourself to face and so you invent me, The Dragon, your own fears made manifest—but please know this: the wind that blows through the orange blossoms and whips this child's gown and hair also cools my nostrils and scales and bones and it blows behind me into the cave, where I have laid and hidden a thousand and more eggs, and that same wind blows, like belly breath from my own body, outward over the chained child and beyond her into the entire known world, including you, who come armored in far less metal than I have hoarded in my caves yet still you charge.

Dear sir, I beseech you, as I unfurl my wings and take a great breath, lower your weapon and embrace me for I am you and even if you kill me today I will be resurrected, a phoenix rising in flames, hissing from within the darkest recess of your heart.

## Cleolinda, 14,
## Pagan, Virgin, & Princess

Though I have always dreamed of Leptis Magna and its
statuary and mosaics and circus and amphitheater and
of floating naked in the Mediterranean and bending the world
to my will, I never imagined my father would sacrifice me to
certain death—I did know that he would sell me to the high-
est bidder, to whoever had the greatest army or the largest
estate or the most power, use me as a mere string to tie a knot
between two kingdoms—I always knew this, the same as I know
that every lady-in-waiting who has attended me, combed my
hair or fluffed my pillows or polished my shoes, wished in
her secret heart to be me, the doted-upon princess—to be the
lone child of King Ptolemy and Queen Sa'diyya—to be the
one heaped with diamonds and attention, dressed in the finest
Egyptian cottons and dyed linens, and studied by every woman
who has enough ambition to be jealous—though each of these
maids stands worshipped by every mother of six toiling in the
street with rags on her bones, who ventures off to the market,
the abattoir, the spring-fed well, and returns home to her
brood of indifferent sucklings, her arms laden with a sack of
grain, a shank of lamb, a drawn skein of water, to cook for
a husband who does not hate her, only that and nothing
more—these women, in turn, are both despised and admired
by prostitutes with rut-bruised knees, blistered backs, and
unforgiving aches in the middle of their bodies—yet these
harlots of the street who envy these domestic women's safe
lives, would never worship me, because I am, after all, one of
their own.

This noble fool comes scampering up—body heaving and heavy beneath all that metal—if he kills the dragon and frees me from my chains, I know I will marry him and convert to his god but only if he grants me one favor more: *Good sir of the Royal Order of Christ, slip into my father's chambers and find him sleeping and slit his awful pimp throat.*

# Judicium Dei or Trial by Combat:
## Le Gris v. Carrouges

*In the Last Trial by Combat Ever Decreed by the Parlement of Paris,
Saint-Martin-des-Champs, on Île de la Cité, Paris, France,
December 29, 1386*

# Charles VI, 18,
## Mad King of France

I cherish a good spectacle, the Lord knows I do, tournaments and banners and armor and arms, and I have
entered them myself, the thundering steed between my thighs,
the lance leveled heavy and true, but last night my only son,
three months old and sickly, succumbed and died—Queen
Isabeau is distraught, the fairness gone from her cheeks, the
luster from her hair, and Sir Jean's lady-wife, Marguerite, has
also given birth but does it belong to her husband or Jacques,
the squire she's accused of rape—how can any man know the
truth of such an accusation and so I am proven mortal—the
joy of the joust is not with us today but rather certain death
as in the constant wars with England or my own father or
my own son—today one of my bravest men will die—his body
will be stripped to the skin, dragged naked to the gibbet, and
hung in Montfaucon, where vultures and magpies will feast on
his limbs and eyes—if Marguerite's champion, her husband,
should fail, then she too shall forfeit her life for swearing a
false oath against my Court—God's will be done, she will burn
at the stake and hang in public alongside Jean, the rot of their
flesh on the wind blowing throughout the city—a spectacle,
true enough, but I do not cherish its kind—she is dressed in
black upon a black-draped scaffold as if already in mourning and so too am I—on the morrow I bury the prince and the
land is hard and cold though the earthworm never sleeps—it
crawls through the earth as surely as my mind, with the stealth
and force of ten British armies, and I would destroy him with
a mace if it would not also mean self-slaughter—a tear tickles

my eye and I know it is but the earthworm itself creeping
from its lair, its head probing forth, and I stand and shout,
*Anon, Anon, Anon*—my voice echoes off the high wooden walls,
the throng of viewers, the silent guards, and the priests who
have cleared the field of their makeshift altars and host—what
do we need with God's verdict today?—am I not His earthly
delegate made manifest in law? If so, then why could I not
conjure the truth, why my blasted hesitancy, my dead child?
Damn the earthworm! Lest he be God's chosen emissary
and the blood of a knight may bring about the resurrection
and rapture!

In the center of the field, the grand marshal holds aloft a
white silk glove until all grow quiet and I am leaning forward
out of my box when he shouts, *Laissez le aller!* and tosses the
glove high in the air and I want to leap for it, catch it, and
wipe my face clean, but instead I merely clap and clap like a
child at play.

## Jacques Le Gris, 50,
## Newly Anointed Knight (Gray Coat of Arms)

We have broken our lances and with my axe I've beheaded his horse and Jean fell to the ground and disemboweled mine and so we were on foot until I lashed open his leg, the blood luscious over his thigh—the sun is noon-high and I sweat and stand over the man, whose breath comes like passing clouds—I recall the day I came to her and she raised a hue and cried, *Haro! Aidez-moi! Haro!* till her voice turned raw and blue and I had my desire of her, her hands tied behind her back and she kicked like a good mule and when I took my leave I donned my wool cap, still warm from having been stuffed in her moist mouth—I raise my long sword over my head and watch its tip touch the pale sun and I see a hawk on the wind and archers in the stands and, as I bring the steel down, the marshals by the gates in the wooden walls and poor Jean lying in the dirt like a thing tossed aside—poor foolish Jean bade me be his first son's godfather not knowing I too was his own true father and his first wife took me as her own deep secret until the day she died—which is worse, Jean having no heir to inherit his land or me having a failed father with nothing to hand down? At an early age I swore that by God's cloak I'd make my mark and so I've taken upon my grievance to amass a fortune, to take all the things of this world I've wanted, and now I will have Jean's estate and child as well.

I miss and the steel buries in the sand and somehow I land facedown and his breath is in my ear, the sound as wet and rogue as the heave of sex, and he has me pinned like a woman and I am helpless and he turns me over and pushes his four-inch dagger slowly into my underchin and I feel the blood choke there and throb out of me like *petite mort* and the sun is there and the ramparts are there and the knights and the priests are there and the executioner and Marguerite and Count Pierre and my lawyer and ten thousand witnesses have all gleaned my guilt but God knows from the voice of our confessions that I am innocent of any crime that Jean would not have committed himself.

# Jean de Carrouges, 51,
# Knight (Red Coat of Arms)

In this age-old grunt of combat, my hearing has gone
dull and mute as if I'm underwater, yet still I hear sweet
Marguerite saying again, *He came to me whilst thou were away in
Scotland defending France's honor*, and my mother, *He sent me on a need-
less errand to Alençon*, and my father gone now these many years,
*Your life is but a balance of just and unjust and you are the hinge it matters upon*,
and Count Pierre in the trial I brought against Le Gris, *The
innocence is with my squire*, and the king himself, my liege lord, *I
cannot choose, I will not choose, I shall not choose*, a whole cacophony of
voices drowning the gasp of the spectators when they saw my
flesh open and I stumbled to the ground and began like a crab
to scuttle away—oh Lord, I beseech Thee, do not render me a
cuckold, Thou hast afforded me valor and victory in forty-one
battles but if I lose today, all is lost, my honor will fly and be
hanged with my body—the talk in the Court and courtyards
and market stalls will not be of my steel and of my strength but
only of the gray in my beard and my faithless M, whose father,
'tis true, was a traitor to the Crown, but she is pure, isn't she,
Lord—my living son will no longer be my son, but his, and my
land no longer my land, but his—oh Lord, I've sworn three
oaths to Thee today, called upon Our Lady and Saint George
and praised the Passion all in Thy holy name, amen—
    Le Gris's legs go awobble and he blunders facedown and
I'm on him and I bang open his visor with the pommel of my
dagger and I demand he unburden himself of sin—even as I
push the blade into his soft flesh he says, blood frothing in his

beard, *In God's name and on the damnation of my soul, I have no crime to confess*, and I push the steel in farther and say, *Confess, man*, and he does not and so he dies and I win and I am alone, questioning the nature of Truth.

# Tilting at Windmills: Nicholas v. Quixote

*On the Plains of La Mancha, Campo de Montiel, Spain,*
*March 15, 1565*

Since we cannot change reality, let us change the eyes which
see reality.

～ Maximus the Confessor

## Argus Nicholas the Giant, Ageless,
## in the Guise of a Windmill, from Pallene
## but Now of Spain

The old man is not as daft as he may appear to be—we are,
indeed, the giants that he sees—after Heracles and his
army of fiends destroyed most of our warriors, my surviving
brethren and I pledged ourselves to love, to peace, to song,
and so became courtiers, immense and strong and loud—
alas, we came to this terrain, wide and wondrous Spain, and
soon our melodies attracted Malady, goddess of the plains,
and of the winds and of the rains, who appeared to us as if
from some radiant dream, bejeweled in myriad grains and
draped in olive branches and antlers, and our poems bent
her ear and wooed her heart and she was our dear muse, our
master, our art, and we thrived until her jealous husband,
Freston the Mad Magician, cast a spell that stole our voice
and turned our skin to stone—no more the spinning of yarns,
now only our sails nigh two leagues long twirling over and
over and over again—we stiffened solid as trees receiving the
breeze blown across Sierra Nevada and birds light and shit on
our shingles and the sun burns the lye white off our skin—yet
this old man sees clear the giant I am, the old warrior I was,
and he challenges my statue self—he shouts for me to glance
the way to Heaven's gate before he charges and now it's too
late to turn back and so, in turn, I spin him ass over end or
trim horse over limb and shatter his lance and drop him on
his pants and, as surely as one look from monstrous Medusa
could turn flesh to stone, he has made me quick again.

Would that I had hands and the chance, when the next winds swung my arms low, I'd dust this knight's bottom and lift him high thereafter for he has, sweet prince, reminded me who I truly am.

# Don Quixote, 49,
## Knight Errant de la Mancha

I am not fool enough to believe this windmill a giant,
but what right man would not choose to live in a world
filled with maidens, beautiful and fair, high romance, a dragon's lair, and a chance to earn a king's ransom, compared
with the daily life we live? So I set out with a dry old nag
and this fool by my side to roam the country over, courting
adventure in order to quell the searing fear of death that
is in every man, and poor Panza, he cannot see because he
has no eyes for fantasy, for dreams beyond his monstrous
belly, yet I know these things exist, the same as I know that
God does not, yet there I am weekly at mass, thumbing my
rosary, a devout, praying at each station of the cross, all
because I desire the approval of my own father, who once
my mother had passed locked himself away in the library and
read himself to death, and so too have I consumed my mind
full of fantasy though I will not be my father, pining love-
less and a loon—I know that before me, squat and bright in
lye-washed white paint, is no giant at all, but I will it to be,
and so it is—how can a man who knows he is mad be truly
mad after all, especially one who knows his life draws near
to close and wants nothing more than a moment's pure good
grace—so, *Hie, vale anon!* I spur dear Rocinante on and into
the giant's flailing arms, aware that his time too is at hand
and shall like my father pass from this world.

I smash my wooden lance against his jaw but, like the
Reaper, he grabs my steed and self and sends us over—the world

whirls by like a Bedouin dervish and slams us to the ground and in the distance I see clouds in the shape of buzzards, beautiful and languid and hungry, and just above me, the windmill's slow, eternal spinning hands.

## Sancho Panza, 47,
## Illiterate Squire

Under this unforgiving sun, I sit muleback in the meager shade afforded by a lone olive tree and I pick the fruit and bite and find it bitter. My bile rises for the want of brine. And of capers and of caper berries and of all things pickled and salty. My donkey has white rings around his eyes like a bull's-eye and me without a dart! His head is like a giant shovel, his large jutting jaw like an insatiable maw! Oh what I could eat if I had that hasp: a dozen *bocadillo con jamon y queso de cabra* because I've always loved the bastards. And here's the old man taken leave of his senses while on a service he declared that God has blessed but it's plain to see there will be no *boquerones en vinagre*; no *ajo blanco* with a nubile Mudejar to grind the garlic with mortar and pestle and no bread to sop into it; no bladders of wine at the ready; no Gypsy girl to tickle my feet with rosemary branches, as we moon over my island paradise, where I serve as lord and governor and bring together the Moor and the Jew and the Catholic alike: come friends, one and all, bare your chests and souls and be my guests. My ass is swayed and my belly is bulging with the fat of years and indolence and friendships raised and toasted and gulped. Don Quixote has promised me this sacred *isla de paz*, but now, seeing his broken body lying in the earth, all hope for it is dashed. Shall I leave him, return home to my wife, who waved me a fond farewell, or to my daughter, who is old enough to marry, herself?

True, the old man is little more than bluff and bluster, hot wind and noisy clang, like the time in my hometown when the wind rose and loosed the Santa Maria bell from its

moorings and blew it out the church tower, bats bursting forth
in all directions, the bell and frayed rope fell an impossibly
long time and crashed in the earth, cracked, and let off one
last toll that sounded in the square for nearly one whole year,
the noise caught somehow in the winding streets of the old
barrio, confused and lost, with no way nor want to find its
way home.

# On Moses's Failed Insurrection:
# Unbada v. Cantrell

*During a Slave Uprising outside Baton Rouge, Louisiana,
March 5, 1811*

## Unbada, 28,
## San Domingan Slave on the Picou Plantation

I am awake but cannot flesh out the haints of sleep, as
though my life's become a dream, a shade passing before
closed eyes. I cannot conjure my name nor who I was, and if
I can't, then was I ever? And if not, then what am I now? I
reach for fleeting images—a woman's parting lips, a child's hair
soft against my palm—when an odor comes over me, strong as
pan-tote bacon fat frying in a deep pot, but like something
else too I can't quite call, and there's a roar in my ears like
waves crashing ashore and that smell drives my feet forward;
it is salty as seawater and like everything I've ever wanted—a
hug from my mother, a free moment to drum and enjoy the
one-pot feast—I'm chest-punched, the air exploding from my
body, and the sky tilts before me and I land on my back and
I yearn to lie still and rest here forever but again I sniff that
weird scent on the wind and am up once more, steady shuf-
fling like the insatiable drive of mules, and all of my labors
and all of my loves pass from me  I can't resist this wanting to
know the source of such intense perfume—my feet propel me
and I am trying to say my name, though it comes out only a
moan, and that water keeps roaring in my ears and I am bel-
lowing like a belly-sick sow, wanting an answer to the question
of that smell, and then I see Boss John and that odor becomes
scythe-sharp and I smack my tongue against what's left of my
last meal, whatever it was, grainy remains like mullet roe in
grits, and all I can see in the world is him and his smoking gun,
but before he can fire again, I realize that he is the answer and
I must have him.

# John Cantrell, 37,
## Georgian Overseer on the Picou Plantation

Night drums come pounding my dreams and I stumble from bed into a scene in silhouette lit only by full moon and fire: the plantation owner, harried, dressed in nightshirt and stockings, his wife and three boys flee in a two-horse carriage and the warning bells clang in riot and the barn's burning slap up, and against the high flames, the shades of slaves ride upon stolen horses and I hope they catch their old master, for I'd like to see that bastard dead as well, so I could claim for my own this land he never worked—the air is redolent with cane and burning flesh, and glass breaks in the Big House and flames roar there too—the fools, this revolting breed of island slaves, followers of Toussaint's rebellion in that far-off hellhole, I'll treat the same as I'd have done him: grab my gun and whip too and come to meet this moaning horde. Unbada's the first I recognize, a docile I never thought would take up arms, even if he is Domingan, and it is a shame I'll have to make an example of him, but he is coming at me, slow but insistent, blood slathered across his lips, so I shoot him clear through and I begin to reload the musket, when I see Unbada rise, and the black powder spills over my hand, streaking the scars I earned from lashing slaves, taxing their backs and lack of labor, these lazy beasts too brainless to conjure the brilliance of Christ on the cross, room enough only for thoughts of what hangs between their thighs, and I am ramrodding the ball down the barrel when Unbada grabs hold of me.

## Pharaoh, 33,
## Second-in-Command to Moses,
## Leader of the Slave Uprising

The bay I ride stands sixteen hands high and glows the
color of fire in the field and we ride over slaver and
zombie alike, neither human enough for my taste—Moses and
I spent moons weaving a plan down to the last stitch and I
urged him hold fast to it—set fire to their homes in the black
of the night and mow them down as they flee, all five hundred of us with sickle and shovel moving to a drum-banging
beat  he insisted on the ways of the old country, said, *Cousin, we*
*can't use the master's tools to tear down his house,* and I said, *Master don't*
*own fire and death no more than cannons own war*—there he is among
them now, Moses, a striking figure on horseback with reins in
one hand, a saber in the other, a pheasant plume tucked in
his hat, looking every bit the president at the birth of a new
nation, circling the men who do his bidding, and as if they
were cattle, he drives them on but they trickle by like black-
strap bound for rum—so this then is our revolt in all its slug-
gish progress, gone now our African speed and grace—beyond
him, in the offing, Unbada rises from the earth like the dead
thing he is, a Negro Lazarus, a hole the size of an urn's base
blasted from his body—no longer is he driven by the cocaine to
work the fields, now some other drug possesses him—Unbada
cracks his teeth into the white man's skull and smoke and
screams are all about me and Unbada laps at the slaver's brains
like a dog in a ditch and I bite my lip knowing our flesh is just
as weak and just as strong as Christ's—I can no longer resist: I
heel my horse in a hell of a charge and Unbada eyes me with

that same dull, lustful look—chunks of flesh falling out his open lips—I run my sword through his brain and Moses has come behind me with his horde of lurching dead and they tug at my feet and my horse rears, all slashing hooves and maniacal, and I club two in their relentless heads yet they yank and yank at my ankles until I finally fall, horse and all, and they are on me, moans in their throats, and though I flail about, I pray for the patience to wait till I too will rise, as I know we all eventually will.

# A Black Night in the South:
## Ackers v. McCarthy Sr.

*An Abolitionist Struggle in Kansas City, Missouri,*
*December 19, 1859*

## Ezekiel Ackers, 56,
## Abolitionist Minister at the Sacred Duty Church

He had gall enough to curse John Brown's grave name
on the day he was hanged—I'd follow that man to hell,
go willing as Jesus, where we'd burn in bliss for the sins of this
land and these men and, too, would rise three days hence,
righteous as ever and tested true by God's own counsel—before
my fold I decried him and his slave-holding ilk, and in turn,
he condemned me in the *Beacon,* called my sermons a cancer,
claimed I should be railroaded back to Kansas—come last
Lord's day he sat proud as Satan on my very first pew, smug
with his son in tow, both stretching their legs and propping
one boot heel atop the toe of the other, so I pointed him out
as an asp in the garden and not twenty hours more he quoted
me on the front page of his no-count rag, using my words as
cause for secession, making me his scapegrace—here he come
again, sallying up the Sunday evening walk like he'd no care in
the world but I barred the door to him, held my hands straight
out and called down the wrath of Moses: *This is the spot where you
and your ways shall pass from Earth,* and slapped his face with all my
might and he said, *You'll not have to wait on my response,* and I, *I may
not be the best shot, sir, but God will guide my way, and after you are dead, I
shall make of my body a horn and trumpet the good news and deliver my Negro
children from Pharaoh's bonds.*

So under these dogwoods, not forty yards from my clap-
board church, we measure our paces—I'm still wearing God's
own armor and the glorified have gathered to bear witness to
my redemption yet he fires first—but at what?—the birds in the

trees or, more likely, the good Lord Himself?—my second
takes hold of my shoulders, says, *Sir, the contest is yours*—I shrug
him off and take soulful care to put my shot dead center
through this heathen's heart.

## Alexander McCarthy Sr., 36,
Founder & Editor of the *Missouri Beacon*

I have always admired the sound of a good sermon, the words tippling one over the other, the rhetorical flair of a man in his Passion espousing the poetry of Love. Likewise, it is good to know the mind of your enemy. So I came to this church to search for the words that informed this pastor's beliefs; instead, I gleaned only his zealous self-righteousness. God knows you can't talk pragmatics against a dreamer's ideology. Yet I have tried. I have tried. But when no peaceful accommodation proved practical, we loaded the pistols I keep in my carriage for just such engagements. Truth is, I don't believe in shackling people any more than freeing them. True character is revealed by the aim of your shot and nothing besides— What a lie! What a liar!—I've covered my heart in a thin veil of words to hide the crimes I commit and now I stand waiting for the word and try to spit but nothing comes out of my mouth. I pinch the bridge of my nose and yawn and steady my breathing as I've done in five previous duels. I level my pistol, which, like its mate, I had handmade in Denver five degrees off true, and I compensate for the weapon's dastard defect— I cannot possibly miss from this distance. I rock back and forth and the leaves crunch underfoot and my breath rises like spirits. I have always enjoyed the winter because I can see farther and clearer and I spot the button on the reverend's wool frock where I will bury my lead. Then I see young Lex, who stares at me with those hollow eyes. Lord, I have been too hard on the lad, I know, blistered him with belts and branded him with irons, but only to clean him of the sin vested in his skin from birth, the matricide he can't recall and for which I can never forgive. Yet in a world so dim and mean, I can at least afford him this one moment of Grace—

I aim my charge heavenward and *delope*—I look to my lad to see if he understands, but I am, as if by some magnificent umbilical cord, yanked back to the world's womb. Slammed into the earth, I can't catch my breath, and all about me are the faces of the congregation. They all look exactly like my lad and they sneer and bare their teeth as if they have come to tear me apart.

# Alexander "Lex" McCarthy Jr., 14,
## Witness & Vengeful Son

Father's eyes bore into mine and I recall him washing the lather from my hair when I was yet a toddler, dunking me beneath the warm water and holding me there until my tiny hands flailed against his wrists and when he finally relented, I shot up straight, gasping for air that burned my lungs, only to find his expression same then as now—I understood that what exists in this world does so with his blessing alone—last week I tore the head from a toad and the week before I gutted Widow Tatum's cat with a sharp river stone—ever since I was strong enough to level a rifle, I have shot wild squab and every creeping thing slithering in God's drat earth. This morning I tore a lizard in two to see which half crawled faster and stomped on the losing end, because the killing, and the mercy, is my birthright—why has Father now sent his shot into the treetops, stark and leafless and gray as skeleton bones etched against the dark sky, where crows scatter, cawing through the clouds? And that preacher, fine white hair whipping about his cavernous face, fires a coward's slug that drives Father down, and as he yaws side to side and keeling, I kneel over him, smoke rising from his belly wound and into my face, and I reach to push my finger into the hole when these Bible gnawers crush against me and I sprawl into his arms and Father hugs me and we lift and carry him to Dr. Gregg's where he will lie in his deathbed, jabbering out his head about degrees of truth until I wish him good and gone already.

I know murder when I see it but that was suicide. Still, I'll send word for the preacher to get square with God, because

two days after we lay Father in the ground, I will bury that
man dead as well. I don't understand all their Bible talk—
preacher and Father could quote scripture to argue the Devil
to tears—through all of the beatings he was still my father and
I was tortured less than Jesus by His: I've always been told that
vengeance is the Lord's, but they never said it is His alone.

# Slap Leather: Hickok v. Tutt Jr.

*In the Quick-Draw Duel That Gave Birth to the Wild West,*
*Springfield, Missouri,*
*July 21, 1865*

## James Butler "Wild Bill" Hickok, 28, Abolitionist, Union Scout, & Gambler

Was a time I rode with Colonel Lane and we took shot from border ruffians; or 'at knife fight with Conquering Bear, who I gave the old sockdolager to, till his blood soaked my buckskin britches; or how I bluffed Kit Carson with a two and a seven, my last ducat laid out on the table afore me; or the shootout I had with 'at cockchafer McCanles at Rock Creek when he bullied me as I mended the stamina I allers had; or when I ran the skirmish line at Wilme Creek and a dozen Johnny Rebs shot my way at'wonce, somehow, God only knows, missing me each and ever time—now here's square-fisted Tutt, the sodbuster in a linen duster, dead set on giving me Jesse—he stands afront of me, thumbing my eye by wearing the Waltham watch my weeping ma give me when I left home ten year ago—I broke her heart on account I thought I'd killed that cunny-fisted Colston boy—I swear, ain't a single damn thing scared me since that black bear in Raton Pass swiped me off my horse and took my six shots in her belly like runaway orphans and tore my shoulder clean out its socket and I even took my Missouri toothpick and stobbed her neck and I stobbed her thigh but she clean tore my head wide open, took my scalp half off like a swinging saloon door, and my fears musta fell out in the rock-strewn dirt, I swear, 'cause right then and right there I was reborn, fearless, and I buried that blade in her heart and killed her graveyard dead, I did.

My trigger finger taps the pistol butt as calm as turning a trump—there are so many ways to die, I reckon a man oughta

consider hisself lucky, notorious at the least, to celebrate these
victories over Death—specially, when it gets told and retold,
if he'd shot twenty-four border ruffians with only six bullets, killed the strongest gotdang Indian chief with but his
bare hands, or had the hair on his ears singed off when ever
durn two-bit Reb shot his way at'wonce—they all wanted me
affrighted but really what is there to fear? Nothing, 'cept
being forgotten and I don't reckon that's gonna happen to
me neither: so buck up, Tutt—you ain't got to grieve too deep
'cause after I kill you here and now, you'll be infamous too,
and I'll be hanged if you won't have been the fastest gun in all
the West, until you met me.

# Davis Tutt Jr. 29,
## Confederate Veteran, Perpetual Sidekick,
## & Gambler

I come out the livery stable to find him cool as Ozark dew
and leanin caddywamp on a pillar of The Lyon House
and I stand tall as can do and open my coat to show his watch
hangin from my fob chain for all who care to see—his bright
blue eyes turn that steel gray they get when his blood is up—he
is a Yankee, Bill is, and I kilt a dozen or more of his kind in
the war but all of em taken together ain't his equal—he and I
rode the ranges this spring and drank the taps dry and I brung
him out to my kinfolk farm where he sweet-talked Sissy and
sneaked off with her to canter rear of the barn and he went
off and did her dirt—before then I'd have torn the eyeteeth
out a wolf's mouth just to get corned with him again—I swear
I wisht I ain't knowed what all he done, so I ain't have to make
this choice here—family or friend, honor or fear—'cause I've
seen him shoot and he is true with a bullet and he got the good
nerve cept when it comes to cards—that tick in his jaw means
he ain't got the trick nor the bluff he shows and so I aimed to
beat him out his bankroll but snatched his watch instead, just
to break his heart a bit, and now he wants this spectacle show
so he hollers across the square and I, I tug my piece from the
holster slung low across my hip and I am in the dad-blamed
war again—brother versus brother—I see my shot bury in the
dirt, spittin up a tornado gainst his moccasins, his thick thighs
in leather leggins, his narrow waist, his broad buckskin-
covered chest, and on up to where the white smoke hides his
hand and hair and fine, fine face:

I am blown clean through and goddamn it hurts—the whole blasted town of looky-loos stares from behind the water troughs and billiard hall windows and saloon doors—*Send for the surgeon, you sonsabitches, don't just stand there stock-still and watch me die*—my scalp prickles and I fall on my haunches, sittin in some mud—who knew I had all this life inside me just waitin to come on out?—my head swoons silly and I close my eyes and feel Bill's hand steady my shoulder and I realize I have often wanted his hand on me and I look up but he is not there and I fall sideways and I just keep falling and falling and

# Dr. Aleister Greggs, 63,
## Former Surgeon, Present Drug Addict,
## & Future Dime Novel Author

I exhale the smoke and a certain peaceful silence blows over
me and I roll to my other side to look through the dingy
lace curtains of Lu Yang's upstairs window expecting the clouds
that attend high noon, but instead the evening sun shim-
mers like a crimson pool on the tin roof of The Lyon, with
its venetian blinds and fancy chipped-ice drinks, and beneath
stands Hickok, the biggest toad in this whole mud puddle,
his fingers all a-wiggle above the hog leg jammed in his red
silk sash—this morning he and young Mr. Davis called on me
as if I were the swamper sent to sweep the sawdust and slop the
spittoons but I storied them on the preacher who I saw shoot
a newspaper man back in '59, who bled to death jabbering
on my parlor room rug—shot him in a duel right in front of
the dead man's boy who later, I heard, gave that clergyman the
short end of the horn—I gave both boys to understand that I'd
not be put upon to clean any more wounds, nor ease the pain
in any way of men who shoot one another, and I assumed that
had settled the score and so we'd have no bloodshed today—
across the square, where flies have gathered on every pile
plopped in the dirt, comes ornery Davis walking down Business
Street, where wagons and horses and mules stand before the
mercantile and blacksmith shops, and he's all squinty-eyed
against the sun, his long coat blowing in the wind, and I conjure in this yellow silence a hawk's shadow inking the earth
between the two men and then the bird screes—I can't get shed
of all the death cries of Quantrill's crazed bandits back in the

war—boys, just boys, slathered in their own gore and I'd ply
them with opium powders till I took a mind to dope myself
and when the war finally stopped I prayed for a certain peace,
but those ghosts speak shadows that never cease nor do they
ever sleep nor disappear.

Their pistols jump together as in a dance and the smoke
rises and Davis spills a mess of blood and collapses into the
mud of his own making and hollers for me to help and Hickok
turns back inside the saloon for a belt of rye, I presume, and
I ease down the water-stained shade on the world and roll
back over and take the pipe to my mouth for one more puff
of God's own medicine, and as though it were the lost souls of
every murdered man I've ever met, I hold that smoke in my
blood and brain and lungs until it burns and has to come out.

# The Black Knight of the South
# (A Gothic Romance): Moran v. McCarthy Jr.

*In the Fourth and Final Duel of the Day
on Bloody Island in the Middle of the Mississippi River,
Near St. Louis, Missouri,
March 23, 1874*

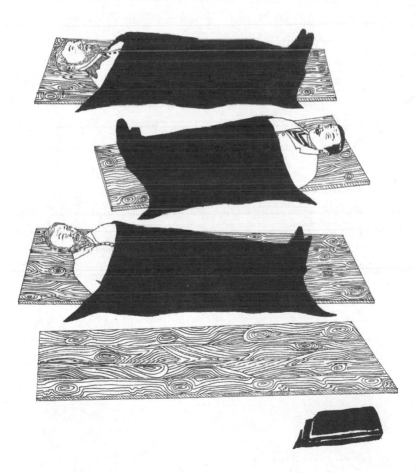

## Cadet Moran, 14,
## Youngest of the Moran Clan

My brain's a dang swarm of bees and that judge just keeps on a-counting and so I count too: my three dead brothers laid out on cooling boards, the color yet in their cheeks; my first duel ever and his fourth today; one bullet in this one pistol in this one life; and six vultures lazy-eighting on the wind, which is God's breath come to cool my skin now as I lick my wrist, thin and clammy. My tongue is pruned. My mouth, cotton. My legs are logs on fire. And the river and the smell it carries from a thousand miles north, is pulled past here roaring like a dad-durn tornado and my numbers go all jumbled and I want to dive in the water and be done with this mess but if I ever wish to look my kin dead in the eye again I must be here to defend Sister's honor and avenge my brothers' deaths—though I've never worked a hard day in my life, instead of these paces I'd rather be walking behind a mule like the tenant farmers who plow our land, or better, digging in the dirt for worms to go cane-pole fishing in Simmons Stream or swimming out there with Jeanette or chasing her through those fresh-turned fields, pulling her ponytail instead of the trigger to this gun that weighs nigh as much as me, but I am here, fingering this cold iron curve, as the judge calls twenty and I stop and spin slow as the seasons change and I see my man and I can't shake the blasts fired earlier today nor the way my brothers bellowed when their blood burst from their bodies, freckling the sand—I clamp my eyes tight as pickling jar lids and the judge hollers, *1, 2, 3, Vale*—

I hear the report clear as church bells but I swear I ain't even squeeze the trigger. I swear. Yet there he is somehow splayed on top of Sister and she's a-kissing his face and I fall to my knees hard in the sand and pray that my brothers now may all rest in peace, though I know I never will again.

## Ms. Mintoria Moran, 28,
## Only Daughter of the Moran Clan

When our skiff struck the shore, I snatched the der-
ringer set beside Doc Reynolds and hopped out the
boat, water licking my ankles, and ran to Mr. McCarthy—my
Alex, my Lex—the wind whispering against my thighs—oh, may
he ravage the world but not my Cadet!—I cannot bring myself
to consider him on a bier beside his brothers, not my Cadet,
brother and nephew and son, born so small and squeaking
in that Natchez nunnery where Father sent me to swell and
whom I carried in, and fed with, my own body—certainly not
now when it is spring and the first crocus fingers have pushed
through the wild moist earth calling for human fingers to
push back—to plant seeds, not bodies—these thoughts go hissing like kettle steam whistling through my mind mingling with
the odor of Lex's skin—that deep scent of sandalwood makes
me a weak-boned six-year-old in Father's lap, wagon-bound
home from market, sacks of vegetables stacked behind us—I
was only going to fire a warning so he might lay down his arms
and take me up in his as he did this morn when I poured his
tea in Mother's fine wedding china—that smell came over me
and my bosom swelled and I swooned and spilled his drink on
the red parlor rug and took his face in my hands and kissed
him hard on his lips and pressed him to me and he pressed me
back, kissing me—John walked in and slapped me and slapped
Lex too—John, the same brother who came to my bed and put
his hand across my mouth and done those things he did and
said it was all my own silly fault—if Lex had killed only John,
or only all three of them boys, I'd still have run away with

him as far as San Francisco—instead he accepted Cadet's challenge with all the passion of a man asked to pare an apple—so
I come to this island for the first time to hear the judge
call *Vale*—

I run yet faster and Lex stares at me and stands still as his
walking stick, his long curled locks black against his bone-pale
skin, his silk-lined cape whipping in the wind, holding that
position like a half crucifix, and of a sudden, he folds his arm
up under his chin and the smoke rises 'round his jaw hasps
even before I hear the shot—his scalp lifts as if he were merely
tipping his top hat to me and he steps back and bows and lists
and falls—I am breathless but there to catch him in my arms,
to rest him in my lap, to put my lips to his moist hair, sticky
with the same garnet that splays across my white skirts, and the
sandalwood smell now couples with an iron taint and he jab-
bers through shaky lips about matricide and marriage and one
night in a castle with a son who should have been killed.

## Alexander "Lex" McCarthy Jr. 28,
### Winner of Nineteen Previous Contests

I stand here again on this towhead spit of land, Father's
etch-handled Manton warm in my hand, my thumb
web tattooed black from all the powder I've spent today—I try
to read my future in the markings but all I see are streaks of
dark chaos, and now this last one, the baby, has come like his
brothers to be brought low by the best shot artist ever known
and it is a shame: during my three weeks here I've admired
this lad, rambunctious and guileless as a baby raccoon, the
kind of kid I might have been if Father hadn't proven himself
coward and damned me to this life of constant killing—though
that's not the truth—I was born a killer, carrïed my mother off
on my very first day of life, and I came to this estate to take
it for my own, to build a castle overlooking the river—then I
met Mintoria—I had to take her too—Cadet could have called
me Father, instead he called for my blood, even though I
put my last ball in his brother's heart and the one before right
through a vest buttonhole, and for the first one, John, I won't
even ask God's mercy—he invited me here, one more specu-
lator to rob, and, as often happens with money and women,
our business ended with a bullet in his eye. I saw him look at
Mintoria, covetous as Amnon, just as I see her now, dainty feet
churning the loam, her skirts held in one fist—and what's this,
a small sidearm in the other—running straight at me. I draw a
line in the sand with the heel of my boot, take careful aim at
her final brother, his eyes slammed shut, and I can go to my
grave certain he too would have fallen on this island—Father
put his pistol skyward and sent me surely to hell—how many

have I killed since then, their faces coming, twisted, to me each night—I can never *delope* nor allow Mintoria to enter this horror of honor and death, so I decide on a thing I've always feared, and the judge hollers, *Vale*—

Knowing there is no shot as worthy as my own, I press the barrel under my chin and squeeze out a prayer—the wind rips through my skull and my bullet carries me into a million falling stars and I'm stretched so far I can't even see my own boots—Mintoria is beside me, pray—I try to explain but I can't 'cause the time has come for me to join my father, Heaven still at a damned remove.

# Catfight in a Cathouse: Carol v. LaRouche

*Two Whores Brawling in a Storyville Brothel
during the Last Month of Legalized Prostitution,
New Orleans, Louisiana,
April 13, 1917*

## Cora Carol, 19,
## Prostitute in French Emma's Circus

Pap sets his lens just so and measures the light and lights
the flambeau and measures again before he duck-
waddles his dicty self back to the camera and whines in his high
nasal voice, *Stay still now, Sistuh*—for the five dollars he offers I'd
stretch his bellows let alone sit here naked on a clean couch—I
shake, laughing, and he says, *Corpse-still now, les ya ruin da print*,
and I wish for a flash I'd been a stillborn and not a trick baby
delivered in this Tenderloin District of men, though they
mean very little to me save the money they bring, like when I
walked in on Ma as she dissolved the purple salts in a washrag
to clean her john who stood there naked and limp, potbellied
and hairy, gazing at me in my white party dress that made me
look even younger than my ten years allowed, and he said, *Why
don't you give your mama a hand?* and I shrugged and took up the
cloth with no more thought than when each Monday I'd take
the gals' bedsheets out—all yellowed with sweat and spilled seed
and Rolly Rye—to scrub and tug them clean, which I did to his
prick and it swoll in my palm, straining against its own fleshy
self, and so I squeezed it more till its top pushed out like some
purple-headed turtle and the man moaned and tangled his
fingers in my locks and tugged my head back till I saw his eyes
closed and Ma guffawed, *Well hell, honey, go on ahead,* and I froze
till she put her warm fingers over mine and we tugged together
only twice more before he spit his load on my forearm, which
I yanked back as if it was snakebit, and Ma laughed hard—hair
and boobies bouncing, head thrown so far back I could count
her cavities—and his grip loosened in my hair and my scalp

tingled good and he slumped down in the chair, fuddled his
drawers midway up, and took from his pocket a five-dollar tip
and Ma come up with a clean rag and said, *Oh my*, and took me
next day to Krauss Department Store where I bought white
gloves and opera-length stockings like any other whore.

Now Vivian crosses the floor—the odor of rain and roses,
all legs and eyes and a sneer spread across her fine face—under
her breath she says, *Bulldagger*, and I've never felt shame for
being a whore any more than for being human, but just now
I feel as if she's caught me diddling myself to a sticky picture
of her split lips, my nipples stiffen and as she passes between
me and the lens, touching her chippie ribbon, I leap from the
couch and snatch that bitch by her long hair and I bang her
against the wall.

## Vivian LaRouche, 15,
## The Flying Virgin,
## Featured Attraction in French Emma's Circus

I walked in the parlor and saw Bellocq acting prissy as a
queen in heat, fluffing a pillow and worrying the knot
in his soft pink scarf, set to make a likeness of ugly ass Cora,
the heavy degenerate—God only knows why, when not one man
I've known has screwed her in the light of day nor lamp—when
he should be making my picture again, because I'm the one
here the men come to see, when in the theater I hang from my
silk ropes, swinging bare-breasted and bewinged above bray-
ing Emma, while she is mounted by her rutting Great Dane,
my braids rising and falling against my pale back, my feet
pointed far out as I can stretch them, admiring my own knees
and thighs and thrush, and I know the men have paid dearly to
watch me and touch themselves—I can't read a lick except that
look in a man's eyes, but Daddy wouldn't even glance my way
when he dropped me here three years ago today—Emma put-
ting that stack of money in his left hand, the tan line precise
from the wedding ring he'd buried with Mother—I'm going
to be a star on the big screen like Lillian Gish or Marguerite
Clark, whose films I've snuck out of the District and into the
Quarter to see, and though I know if I'm caught over there I'll
be arrested or beaten or raped, I will continue to cross busy
Basin and Rampart Streets on down to the Louis Gala House
where they show films for a nickel apiece, and as I sit in the
dark watching their large eyes on screen, I say to myself, *Vivian,
that is going to be you someday soon, and Daddy, I swear, you will have to pay to
see me again.*

As I cross the wide-plank floors, I happen to pull the string of my dress and it comes undone and my chest rises against the lace and pushes it apart and I stare first at Bellocq and then at his camera's one big eye and my lips swell and sweat and begin to itch a bit—does he touch himself when he holds the portrait of my nakedness?—my head snaps back and I'm pinned on the wall with that dyke's breath in my ear and I bite her forearm and twist her chin back and bury my thumb in her eye and we crash to the floor and she's pounding my head into the wood and I wish I had my razor to undo her with, because though I am very small, I am not an easy row to hoe.

# John Ernest Joseph "Pap" Bellocq, 43, Photographer

Cora and Vivian tuggled and tussled and upset the lit
flambeau though I caught it, screaming, *Watch da flames*,
my voice high and shrill like the horror of a baby's wail—*Watch
da flames*, my *parrain* yelled—him, swatting mad with a blanket in
both hands trying to put out the blaze that climbed up Sister's
crib; her, squalling as fire caught her flannel gown and hair;
me, having begged for him to leave the lamp lit while I slept a
bit longer and who in dream-terror of wild worms and rutting
rats in my brain had kicked it over and burnt my baby sister
damn to death—gone now my father and mother and my sweet
big sister too, my only brother off in the ministry—I alone
am left to stand against Death like Madame Josie, the grand
demimondaine, whose portrait I made to hang on her crypt
door beneath the statues of the little girl and the twin pillars
of flame, and though I set her likeness a mere three years
ago, the sun has bleached it back to a silver-slabbed mirror
and now when you visit her memorial you stand agawk greet-
ing your own gape-mouthed visage on the bronze door of her
tomb, which reminds me of my own burial plot—I can see it
from my bedroom window and there too I can hear the pistol
fire from Marcet's shooting gallery and see the government
eviction posts on every building in the District and the paint
peeling off Willie Piazza's mansion in great white swaths long
as funeral tunics—all this after I've returned from my pleasure
at Anderson's Annex where the boys belly to the hand-carved
bar and snook schooner after schooner of beer under the
one hundred electric bulbs blasting the dark back in a blaze of

white light, but up in my room it is quiet and dim and I wash my face in the basin and remove my clothes and put on my nightshirt that smells clean from powder and climb into bed to sleep with the lamp lit beside me.

Cora and Vivian continue to wrestle, both now nude, and they spill onto the sofa like champagne outflowing its flute and in a flash I uncover the lens and shoot their picture even though I know full well the glass will not contain their image any more than our bodies can hold our souls and the portrait will be a blur, a pale smear like smoke rising dark against a darker wall or like cotton sheers billowing in an open window, because nothing here ever lasts.

# Shanks in the Courtyard: Ramirez v. Nu'man

*In the Yard of the "Walls" Unit, DOC Facility,*
*Huntsville, Texas,*
*February 13, 1962*

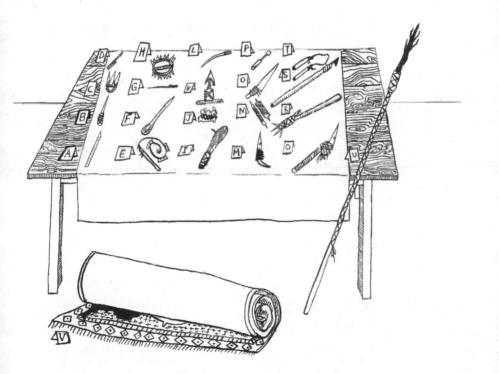

## Miguel Ramirez, 21,
## d.i.n. 59-68-11,
## Convicted of Manslaughter, Serving Twenty to Life

In last fall's rodeo, during the Hard Money Event, I went between the bull's horns to grab the cash bag while two other boys got gored and carted off in the old meat wagon—I took the 1,500 bucks and the wild-headed applause of forty thousand strong—since then every swinging dick in here has asked me for stamp money or fags, candy bars or stag rags—I been racking up favors enough to be mayor of this joint, 'cept from this punk here who runs the commissary, how I knew he's the one that ganked my dough—I can't let him go with that, so I got my boy D-Train to make me a shank wrapped at the base in shoe lace and boxing tape and I been just waiting to find him alone in the yard—there he is now, bow-headed and kneeling on some A-rab-looking rug, and though the sun is out, ice still clings thick on the chain-link fence and when it catches the light, the razor wire looks dead-on like glass and my breath twists from my lips like the cigarette smoke that rose out Papi's mouth the one and only time I saw him—he was leaning against Nguyen's liquor store with his hair creamed into waves, 'stache trimmed pencil thin, dark skin peppered with darker freckles—we two looked like tomcat and older tomcat—I had all these things I wanted to ask or say or to hear him say to me but I gummed up, mouth dry as an old lady's snatch, and a vomiting sissy feeling seized my guts and my voice shrank so tiny I couldn't speak—I just stood there like a dummy till this white gal came out, a pint in a brown bag, and took the Slim cherried between her thin lips and put it right into his gold-tooth smile and he sucked as deep as I do now to steady my nerves and he blew circles past me, like I circle this thieving punk here, and Papi winked at me, as this metal winks in sunlight, and then he was gone and that was the end of me for him—but for me, it was just the start: I went home and put my thumbs into the throat of the sleeping man who'd called himself my dad for eighteen brutal years—

And I have to live forever knowing I strangled the wrong motherfucker.

## Muhtady Nu'man (a.k.a. Ant'Juan White), 38, d.i.n. 48-12-67,
## Convert to Islam, Convicted of Murder,
## Serving Life without Parole

I am chaste, I am devout, and I have no doubt that Allah is love—He makes the grass green and the sky blue— though they have bound my body behind bars, my mind is free from this racist power structure—survived in here eleven years and kept clean, studied my Qur'an, and lived one day at a time—converted to the True Way when I learned what a trap it is to be black in America—tried to hip youngblood to this knowledge but he called me eight shades of nigger— his slave mind holds him like a harness—he's sworn to take my life over the white man's money that his own braggarty boys robbed him of one dollar at a time—my ablutions per- formed, I stand, *Sami 'allâhu-liman hamidah. Rabbana wa laka-l- hamd*—we brothers have killed enough of each other, still I stole a soup spoon from the staff dining hall, filed it down on my cell wall till the handle was needle sharp, packed the bowl full of clay, wrapped it in upholstery for a bet- ter grip, and wear it stuffed inside my waistband where it presses against my belly as I face Mecca for the second time today—his shadow runs cold on my side and I spin, shank in hand—he gouges my neck and I can't work my jaw or hands, my weapon is gone and I collapse and think of Allah—*Cry your tears on me, O Lord, Your humble, faithful servant*, but there is only white clouds in a cold blue sky and I am forsaken: there's nothing in life but cloud and cold sky and this last regret:

I am a thieving junkie in an alley off Liberty Street—I hide behind a Dumpster in a spitting rain, like a rat pressed greasy-backed against a brick wall, holding some old lady's vinyl purse—above me there's a woman on a covered balcony and she's missing both her hands, nubs alone, yet her eyes shine as stars—she is the Nubian beauty of sculpted shoulders and long black legs—I stand from my shadow and she looks down on me and I am high and low at once—in her eyes I see my future until there is no more of it but I do not speak and now I am dead in this yard—yet her eyes look down upon me once again and I see she is Allah's messenger and she is whole again, sent to make me whole as well, and her godly hands part the sky in two like veils drawn back and she is love and God is love and she is calling me to Heaven to be amid love forever and I am gone.

# Douglas Wascom, 33,
## Prison Guard for the Last Seven Years

These men have committed murder before and I figure
one will kill at least one man more but if I were
in charge of being in charge I'd set em both in Old Sparky's
lap, flip the switch, and light em up, but it looks like they've
gone and killed each other already and a circus erupts, two
gangs wilding like the time Johnny Cash played here and
sang that line, *I shot a man in Reno just to watch him die*, and the men
got so jazzed they damn near rioted, blacks and whites alike
howling and shoving and just like then I go to swinging my
baton, clipping hamstrings and smacking skulls, when the
stick bounces off bone, it vibrates through my knuckles and
wrists and into my shoulder jambs—I find myself alone at the
center of the sour-smelling fray, my billy club useless as a wet
match with bodies pressed against me and where are the other
guards?—I hear their whistles far off bleating lame as lambs
in the field, hear a shank click my spine, a tiny sound like the
lock on a window turning—the Dominican stands before me
dumb, a shank jammed in his tiny left ear—I feel the blades
biting me all over now and I flop to my knees, hold my arms
up for mercy, steam rises from my wounds, blood rolls over
my sleeves, and a flood of images, as if from a Kodak carousel,
flashes before me:

*Caught light in moving glass—jump blues on the crackling radio—Pa in my
window, holding a finger to his lips—me in footy pajamas padding behind him—
the hallway lined with clocks and black and white photos of people I'd never
meet—the dark shadow with Ma in bed—a burnt sugar smell—the name,* Luke,
*in Ma's mouth—my neck hair standing on end like electric peppermint and the*

*wind blowing the curtains about like drunken dancers—a pistol miraculously in* Pa's hand—I lie beside this dead Muslim with his dead Muslim eyes staring deadly at me, our blood soaking into the same rug—*the pistol roaring—smoke and dim moonlight in the window frame—* Johnny Cash—*Ma screaming on the front porch, her nakedness covered in a bloody sheet—Pa in handcuffs and in that squad car—a dead man in the bed— Ma dead now from her vodka and pills—*and me in a prison—I'm soon to join them all, my blood on this holy rug—*my eyes on that man's eyes—*my eyes on this man's eyes—my, oh my oh my.

# Code of Conduct: Frato v. Greene

*In White City Park Beach, Cleveland, Ohio,*
*November 26, 1971*

## "Big" Mike Frato, 37,
## Garbage Man, Husband, & Father

M e and Danny go way back, used to be best pals, named
my son after him and he called his Mike after me, but
I didn't work my fat ass off day and night to build a company so
his goons could strong-arm me, take my hard-earned money,
and not kick a thing back—I got fourteen kids to feed and now
he wants to be one mouth more, but it ain't Danny's mouth got
me riding shotgun with a pistol in Palladino's Riviera, creeping
up behind him as he jogs in this park, my hand hanging out the
window, wind burning my knuckles a deep purple—the cracked
vinyl dashboard crimson against the white exterior of the car and
the world and the sky—I told Danny *No*, and *Hell no*, so last month
he sent Art, his right-hand man, to blow up my house with a
bomb, but Art got the chickenshits and ratted me their plan, and
he must have spilled to Danny too, because three nights later Art
exploded all over my Susan's car, our children rattled from their
nearby sleep—blew one of Art's shoes into our neighbor's Douglas
fir and it hung there like some sort of Christmas ornament.

I've always loved the trash business, moving what's unwanted
to somewhere far off—in my first year driving a garbage truck
I found a dead guy's maggot-filled corpse in the hopper—I
told the cops and they pinned it on some made guy from
Youngstown and my dad said, *Don't go getting your nose all wet*, and,
*A dead man ain't got no name*, but what does he know about being
a man, that deadbeat who ditched us ten kids and now comes
groveling for cash once or twice a year—my mom, she worked
three jobs to keep us under one roof and always told me, *A real
man don't need no gang because he can always do for himself.*

## "Unkillable" Danny Greene, 38, USMC, Gang Leader, & Single Father

Five hundred push-ups, five hundred sit-ups, two hundred pull-ups, and enough squats to burn my thighs and now I'll run ten miles more—I need to punish myself so I can punish others—and later the Bushmills will taste even better as it burns the back of my throat—the whisky's my final vice—I've gone vegan except for the fish-oil pills, and instead of cigs, there's tofu and spinach, beans and carrots, and there's no more speed just exercise and vitamins and the thrills of fists and bones—keep the pasta away, stay slim and strong and flexible, because you have to be nimble, Danny boy, in this line of work—stay strong as my ancestors, those Celtic warriors, 'cause soon as I rest some Guinea's gonna put his bullet through my ear or a bomb in my car—my Saint Jude medal flapping against my Adam's apple can protect me only so far—breathe, man, fill your lungs with the searing air and feel the blood in your veins—the thin snow crunches under my sneakers, the wind burns my face red, I am freezing and winter's only just begun—my lips are chapped and I remember, as a longshoreman, the pain of shoveling tens of thousands of pounds of grain in bitter cold like this, until I saw the sit-down job was the way for me—in a window up on the hill I see an Irish angel, stark red hair and emerald negligee, and she is staring straight at me and she will be my guardian as sure as my name is the Unkillable Danny Greene.

I hear a car humming behind me—I know there's someone in it who wants to see me dead but good luck with that, lads, because I may have been born with no name, "Baby Greene"

it says on my birth receipt, but damn it all if I haven't earned
my name by now—I spring through a row of boxwood bushes
on the side of the road, hit the ice-hard ground, and duck and
roll as they trained me in the Corps, pull the piece from my
waistband, and come up firing—yes I believe in charm and luck
and a host of superstitions, but sometimes you have to make
things happen your own damn self—I pushed the button on
Art's bomb but I was around the corner when it went off, so
maybe it was bad timing or faulty wiring or his own fuckup—
staring at these two dead men now, my heart racing but my
hand steady as a shillelagh, I know I've just killed another close
friend but who wouldn't call either self-defense?

## Cathy Summerall, 36,
## Unemployed, Single, & Mother of One

He's coming up the hill toward me, same as every morning, nine o'clock sharp, with that body and them muscles
and his butt tight in green track pants, you bet I'm gonna
watch him run—the snow falls all around but never seems to
touch him—his breath comes in clouds and those ruddy cheeks
and strawberry-blond hair remind me so much of Joey and his
beautiful mechanic hands, always black-nailed and smelling
of diesel, resting on my shoulders, a comfort at my mother's
grave, the press of those hands on my hands as we buried my
father, and later, he would squeeze my entire bicep in one
hand and when he'd let go, the blood would rush to my skin
and I would immediately miss his touch—Joey's lips on my
lips deep kissing in White City Park Beach, the feeling of him
spooned up against me, his hand cupping my growing belly—
little Tyson swelling in my body, pressing against my bladder,
and the pressure of giving birth, a pain beyond pain that I
recall as if through a veil of gauze, and now the pressure of
rent due on the first and Joey, that sad sack, doing a hard ten
for stealing Snap-on tools from the Triple M—Tyson needs
formula and Tyson needs diapers and maybe the rumors about
this running man are true, that he gave turkeys to every beat
cop in town and two to each orphanage—maybe this Danny
Greene can float me a loan for a few bucks, and for his faith
and interest I could pay back his interest and faith with a good
old-fashion lay.

I'm leaning against my front window, the cool glass
against my cheek, when a long car pulls up behind him with a

man hanging out the window—Danny does a somersault into the winter gem, and when he comes up, I hear two pops, like swatting flies with a rolled-up newspaper, smoke rises from his pistol like the breath from his lips, and I see holes and spidered lines across the front windshield and blood spattered all over the side of the door and down into the white snow and the car careens into my apartment sign and stops, the horn blaring in the silence, and I am frozen as the ice on Erie, watching Danny lean into the driver's window, shaking his head grim-like, and he looks up and sees me and I catch myself smiling in the reflection of the glass, the cigarette smoke twirling languid between my two fingers that caress my collar-bone and I know the gossip is true—the beatings, the bone breakings, the bombs—I know now he's going to need me too and now I want him even more.

# It's a Family Affair: Sellers v. Sellers

*In Dr. Matthew's Office for Couple's Counseling, Dubuque, Iowa,*
*September 20, 2006*

# Louise Sellers, 8,
## Third-Grade Daughter of Warring Parents

This place smells like Lysol and there are no toys or books and on the one TV they're showing *This Old House* and the sorrow sob starts to bobble my chin and I've cried all week and no one has cared—not Mommy, not Daddy—because show and tell was Monday and last Sunday night I was sitting in the tub singing "Ducky Duddle" when all of a sudden, *Oh gripes, it's tomorrow*, so I hopped from the tub all lickety-split, pruned and wet and sudsy, but Mommy's door was shut, like always, and Daddy was looking over numbers, not listening to me—I tried to tell him how important the assignment was and all he came up with was our science experiment, which I thought was a dumb idea but what else could I do? He took down from the window sill the glass jar where we kept the carrot chunk and the roots were all white and going everywhere like if an octopus's legs were made of lightning and it did look pretty cool—*You can show them how their food grows; that's interesting, isn't it, dear?*—I was happy to show it off at school but when the bell rang and I got to class and I pulled the thing out, Marcy Dungee said, *Eww, what's that?* and Monica Dowell laughed and Melissa Dunhill said, *That looks like your hair,* and Misty Duncan snorted and shook her long red curls and pulled a Cloe Bratz doll from her Hannah Montana backpack and Melissa her Game Boy and Monica her new ruby bracelet that sparkled all bedazzled and Marcy her whatever and then Tommy Ewland said, *What, are you, like, poor or something?* and Marcy said, *Ewwwww*, again, but this time with that nose whine she does so good, and my chin started bobbing and I buried my head in my arms down on my cold desktop so no one would see my lips shake—it wasn't like last year when Tommy's little brother was run over by the school bus and I made sure everyone saw me crying the most so they'd know I was Tommy's best friend, and the tears ran down my face and I made a big show of wiping the snot on my velour sleeves and leaving the tears on my face so everyone could see how truly sad I was but this past Monday I felt as if some weird bird had pecked out my guts and I blame it all on my stupid dad and my stupid mom too.

I hear her start to yell and cry and I hop down under the big wooden table and grab my knees and curl them to my chest and rock back and forth like I do at home whenever I am scared—like during big storms or when in the middle of the night you wake up and it's just too quiet and the only sound you can hear is your own heartbeat and you think, *When will this ever end?*

# Dannyelle Louise Sellers, 32,
## Former Beauty Queen, Current Housewife,
## & Mother of One

When Billy was president of the Chamber of Commerce and I was on stage in my Aldo heels and Naired legs and a swimsuit so white that my torso glowed at the center of my dark limbs, I was the object of his desire but now he doesn't even look at me—I know it's not his fault that he's never been able to truly see me because, though I was in that pageant, I was not really even there—how could I have been?—I stood on that stage a prancing six-year-old in front of my mother's armoire, running my hands over the hanging cashmere and rayon and jersey denim dresses and over her sweaters and skirts, the grays and beiges and taupes, and in her bureau drawers among her bras and her panties, frilled and laced, and the black silky slip that I'd put over my towhead locks and let flow down my back like long black hair, and in which I'd swish and sway and say, *Oh Captain Smith, save poor pitiful me from this life of a savage*—her hard crenellated vibrator came to life in my tiny electric hands with pink-painted nails just as Mother walked into her bedroom—she put both her hands to her mouth as if to stop a smile but she did not smile—*Just what do you think you are doing, young lady*, she asked—*I'm being you, Mom*—and she slapped my face to burning—*The hell you are*—her face was hard and severe and I stammered, *I guess, I guess, I'm being Pocahontas?*—she slapped me again but harder—*You think I'm some kind of goddamn Indian whore? You are nothing but a—*

He calls me *beautiful* and I call him a liar and shift in this microfiber chair, the backs of my legs sweating even in the artificial cold of this office, because who is beneath this layer of powder and rouge, this four-layering eye shadow, this gloss and lipstick and lip liner, this bobbed blond hair and these earrings, I don't know—peel back this mask and who is there—in that Motel 6 in Grand Rapids you promised me the Ms. Corn crown but all I really wanted was someone to see who I truly am and to tell me, though the only way I know how to ask it is by smiling broad, Vaseline smeared across my teeth.

# William Sellers, 42,
## Jeweler, Father, & Unfaithful Husband

Six Saturdays in a row, D's dragged me here to listen to
this so-called doctor talk about trust issues and accep-
tance and respect but I am not the one who closed the door on
this marriage, clamped it tight as a chastity belt, and for all the
money this doctor charges you'd think she'd offer me a scotch
or at least an orange juice freshly squeezed between the knees
of a sixteen-year-old Filipino girl and the doctor asks why am
I smiling and I say, whimsical-like, *She's the most beautiful woman
I've ever known*, which is true, or at least was true, especially when
we'd walk along the summertime banks of the Mississippi,
her long legs drawing every man's eye, and I was not middle-
aged then and there was not the pressure of employee health
insurance and a child and retirement and savings, just our
hand-holding strolls—that was back before D let herself go,
and suddenly she says, *You're such a liar*, and my face flushes and
before me I see Peggy through the small window of my office—
she is standing at the counter showing earrings to a customer,
Peggy's narrow hips and long waist, and she looks back over
her shoulder and I am caught, but she winks, blows a pink
bubble with her gum, and smiles with the dark shade ringed
around her ruby lips and I'm a fool sitting at my bench re-sizing
some heifer's wedding ring and now there is hail raining
against Peggy's metal window awnings, the sound ringing in
our afterglow, the window unit in her double-wide hums, and
her panties ring her ankle, one shoe still clings to that pale
foot, the salt smell cologned about us—my own wedding ring
in the glove box of my new Boxster—the ring around the tub

where we made love all last winter and Henry the dachshund runs rings around the playpen and *Tiny Toons* is on the TV even though her kid passed away two years ago and she told me yesterday that I said I'd leave D but I don't remember ever saying so, or even believing that, though I can see my marriage is dead as dead can lie, ring around the rosies dead, but I am not willing to lose little Louise or half my things, like my fine jewelry or my red convertible that wooed Peggy to me in the first place—pudging and balding, skin loose about my jaw—and D says, *Damnit, I want out of this life*, and I repeat her, *You want me out of your life*, and she says, *No, I want out of this life*, and I say, *That's what I said*, and we start to argue again and yell and we both see the light of freedom yet neither of us is willing to let go of this darkness.

# PART III: ✝ SATISFACTION

# Delivered into His Hands: David v. Goliath

*In the Valley of Elah,*
*1025 BC*

David, 16,
Eighth Son of Jesse, Bethelemite Shepherd,
Poet, & Musician

I was in the southern pasture among my lambs and fer-
tile fields, chanting dirges to the dead, when an angel
of the Lord, white and ethereal, came upon me and said,
*Behold, David, King of the Israelites*, and I shivered and my heart
was quickened and I said, *I only want to sing songs to my living Lord,
psalms of devotion, psalms of praise*, but it said unto me that the
Lord had chosen me even before I was born—there was
indeed no choice to be had—I laid out my harp alongside
my staff and took up my sling to the field of war—I do not
fear for I have already smote a bear and also a lion—as if
the angel could read my very mind, it said unto me, *His holy
aim was true even then and shall remain steadfast unto this day, young
king, and He will protect thy flesh also from harm*, and I went into the
brook banked by cedar and by juniper and the water was cool
about my feet and ankles like the cold compress Mother laid
upon my forehead as I raged feverish and demented in bed,
thinking surely this was death but it was not death—instead it
was the first time the angel came before me and spoke and I
could see the light of the Lord even as I shivered and raged
and when the angel left my side, the burning left my flesh as
well—now I run my fingers across the smooth stones of the
brook bed and pluck them as if they were strings upon my
harp and I hear a music that shakes my bones, and though I
am little, my wrists and ankles are large, my feet and hands
are large—I take up five rocks and deliver them from the
brook bed, as I have delivered the lamb from the bear and

also the lamb from the lion, and I put them each one by one into my pouch and my body is covered in sweat and I dip my head into the cool water and it plays over my hair and into my scalp and rolls down my neck and spine and I stand straight and say, *Lord, show me the way.*

# Goliath, 39,
## Twelfth Son of Abimelek, Half Giant,
## & Philistine Warrior of Gath

*N*o *man like me, no man like me,* I overturn your temples,
uproot your largest tree, I thump my breast covered in
bronze and it resounds with a gong and the armies behind me
answered after this, chanting, *No man like you, no man like you—*
I pace before the very army of Israelites and I am bereft of
arms, only my hands calloused from long hours of grappling
these runts—*Which man among you will yield himself to me, will have the
sincere audacity to stand before and not wither like the dry vine, the grains of
time slipped through the hour glass?* They are sore afraid and dismayed
and I am elated because my ribs still ache from the blows I
took last time I saved my puny men from certain death—our
gods of iron have left us in this waged war, hidden, not to be
found—I cannot fight them all for I am but half giant, not the
full-flung fury of my father and half brothers—alas, I am but
ten feet tall, my uncut mansword a mere cubit by my hand's
measure—I am tired and I will not be able to save us again—I
shout them down to scare them away, *Let's have him quick and be done
so I may return to the fun of sleeping with your wives and eating your children,*
and then he comes:

A mere boy in a loincloth, comely and soft—his armored
brethren deride him as did my own half brothers me—full
giants, they used to jeer and kick at me as they held my wrists
and made me slap of my own face and said, *Why are you hitting yourself, Goliath? Why are you hitting yourself?* And I'd cry and
try to hit them back but they'd palm my forehead, their arms
impossibly long, I could never reach them with my fists even

as I'd swing and swing and swing—I called after the boy in this manner, saying, *Come to me and I will give thy flesh unto the fowls of the air and to the beasts of the field,* and in turn I hear him say, *I come naked save for my Lord of Hosts who shall deliver thee unto my hands,* and he begins winding his sling above his head, each time it passes it appears as some god's winking eye, and then he grunts and lets it fly.

# Ephram of Gath, 17,
## Only Son of Mutawadd'i,
## Philistine Slave, & Shield Bearer

I have stood beside Goliath each of these last forty days, his armor bearer, his boy with spear and shield—I have no choice in this state, I have been made his indentured servant—true, I stole a sack of acma to feed my starving child and I was caught bread-handed and the priests punished me thus—we have thousands more men than they but our courage has flown and we do not march on their army, instead we parade this one hulking hector to shame them into submission and who can fault them their fear—then comes the boy, unarmed save a sling in his hand and a song on his lips, and he is ruddy and goodly to look upon and everyone goes so quiet, verily, you can hear his footfalls in the sand and he calls to Goliath with a wave of his hand and Goliath turns and I hand him his spear and I hand him his shield and his sword is sheathed and his shadow is long through the valley—the wind kicks sand into my eyes and the boy whips a stone that catches my man in the leg and shatters his knee, but before he hits the ground, the boy has rushed upon him and unsheathed Goliath's sword and, in one poetic gesture, brought it down upon his neck and, in this endeavor, severed the giant's head and freed me as well and the clouds part and a great stalk of light strikes me full on and I fall prostrate and repent my many sins and this boy touches my spine with the tip of the sword and I right myself, speechless, as he hefts Goliath's head by its hair and his army rushes forth on all sides like floodwaters bursting a river's bed and my godless army flees, impotent and ashamed—I embrace this boy's legs and kiss his feet for I have found my king and I have found my God.

# Dueling Visions of *David*:
# Donatello v. Michelangelo v. da Vinci

*Florence, Italy,*
*1440–1505*

For the Lord seeth not as man seeth; for man looketh on the outward appearance, but the Lord looketh on the heart.

— I Samuel 16:7

# Donato di Niccolò di Betto Bardi
## (a.k.a. Donatello), 54,
### Creator of Bronze *David*, 1440

He need not be muscular nor strong as the classical nudes but in fact can be effeminate and small as Giovanni when he sweeps the shavings from the studio floor—his sandals and hat are comely as are his long curled locks and his jutting round belly, so like a woman fresh with child, and my *David* is a child too, a shepherd from the field—it is not his might and brawn that win the day but rather his courage and faith that God invested within him—even the meek can inherit the earth if God is but within them—I have made him proud over the vanquished villain but I shall not circumcise him no matter the Judaic law because Giovanni's lovely member is still intact and often on display as he models for clay drafts in my drawing room, the light coming through the high windows as dust motes dance about us, and we are done for the day, the drawings have been made and the models completed—the room is clean although we are lousy with sweat and debris and I towel him off and he towels me off and we lie beside one another on the featherbed above the straw mattress, where I often go for inspiration, and we close about us the curtains, and though the Florentines have banned *luxuria*, I shall not be bound by their laws or their art and so I have created something new, something built upon no known paradigm, and the Medicis can refuse their patronage, rescind their money—they can take this bronze back and melt it down, bust it, hide it away forever, but I will know what I have created here and I will be my own man despite the thousands they've persecuted for love—the smoke from my tinderbox envelops us as we ignite a fine fire and recline, warm and safe in my studio, and as far as I'm concerned, the Medicis are the giant, the powerful, the obese, and I am the mere naked boy who has conquered it, put my foot on its decapitated head, and yawned, even as its beard tendrils tickle my leg and beg my attention.

## Michelangelo di Lodovico Buonarroti Simoni
## (a.k.a. Michelangelo), 29,
## Creator of Marble *David*, 1504

As a child, I hiked among the snow-dappled ash and maple and beech of the Alps and ran my hands over the contours of rock and thought, *Rain is the greatest artist*, but now I see that idea as but the folly of youth, my enormous ignorance alone saved me from blasphemy—rain is but a tool wielded by the Great Practitioner, just as I use mallet and toothed chisel—those behemoth rock formations unknown centuries in the making, chipped away one wet drop at a time—oh, the patience of the Creator!—the images they hold still not apparent to us mortals—and that is the hell in dying—all that unfinished work I will never live long enough to realize—so when I saw my *David* trapped within the Meseglia stone, I knew it was my God-given duty to carve and coax him free, to birth and deliver him, and by pitching large portions of unwanted stone, I began to take away everything that was not of his form until this final figure remained, coolly posing in contrapposto just before he enters battle as I did with my mentor, old Ghirlandaio, who refused my wages but whom I have conquered and surely surpassed—my *David* lives forever on the hinge, a coil of potential movement, the moment before his immortality—here is a man who has made a conscious choice and will soon spring into conscious action like I with hammer raised over rasps and rifflers, abrading the stone into folds, and with a sand cloth I made him fine and smooth and polished him until the marble was as silken as a woman's armpit hair and about me there lay chunks of debris and white powder fine as ash—

I think of the many friends I have lost to the grave due to plague or war, the many I have forgotten because of my negligence or overindulgence, my family back in Caprese— my mother and father to whom I send every cent I earn—and Sofia, sweet Sofia, who took to a nunnery in Rome rather than to my adulterous bed—now, in the middle of all these people come to crowd about the Palazzo della Signoria just to see my statue, I am left with these fading images and I am become more wholly at home in the realm of God—I exist as though a spirit until I find myself with pitching chisel in hand and then I am made God's errand boy again, sent to find the figures hidden in the stone, and with each stroke I earn my place in Heaven where God's hands will envelop me, hide me for eternity, where only He, the ultimate artist, will be able to divine my self secreted within the stone.

## Leonardo di ser Piero da Vinci
## (a.k.a. The Renaissance Man), 53,
## Creator of Various Charcoal *Davids*, 1505

I know he knows of my trials, the attempts to put me in
chains with claims of sodomy—even though I was acquit-
ted, he looks at me askance as if he sees me as Donatello's
*David*, effete and limp but a hero nonetheless, because I've seen
him admire my *Annunciation*, my *Last Supper*, my *Vitruvian Man*,
with as much intensity as I have attended his sculpture, stood
at its feet night and day and run my hands over its marble until
I felt its warm bones beneath and its blood quick in the veins,
and any man who could make that perfect male form must also
have within him the same love and longing as I—yet no matter
how long I sketched his sculpture I could not find its grace.

Would that I were craftsman enough to complete the
triumvirate—three *Davids* of Florence facing south and staring
down Rome, the giant—instead I merely sat scribbling these
drawings and that is my shame—I cannot meet his measure—
oh, that I could give my *David* the supple, fluid qualities of
Donatello's—whose body is nimble and shows God's good
grace—and the hard, torqued strength of Michelangelo's—
whose body is perfect, thereby reflecting the perfection of his
character—I had such a plan to put mine between the two, the
bridge between the thought and victory, the stone just leaving
his sling, his body twisting like this smoke about me, the man
in action.

Yet I have set each of my charcoal sketches afire though I
know paper cannot burn—it must first be altered in substance,
changed from solid to gas, so then it may burn—I do not

mention these ideas for fear they'd incarcerate me for heresy but I've witnessed long enough my studies transforming into ghosts of their former selves, spirits that ignite and vapors that flame—fifty-one studies in all going up in the blackest smoke, twisting and twirling like David in action, phantoms rising out the chimney, and so I burn them all but one, my love letter to Michelangelo.

# A Prediction Come to Pass: Gabriel, Comte de Montgomery v. King Henry II

*On the Grounds of the Place Royale in Paris, France,*
*June 30, 1559*

## Gabriel, Comte de Montgomery, 29,
## French Nobleman & Captain
## in Henry II's Scots Guards

In my heart I have already converted—what use have I of
pope or any other intercession—I love the king, I swear I
do, but I do not love his ban—I bite my tongue and hear my
heart pound under this armor—sweat runs in sheets down my
back and my hair mats against my skull, my mouth dry and
my wineskin empty—I ask my squire for the wooden-tipped
lance, the kind they used in olden days—the banners of peace
are blowing about us and they are in riotous celebration,
musicians and dancers, a makeshift abattoir where oxen and
lambs are slaughtered—hawkers and draught pourers, jugglers
and dove sellers—so it should be, King Henry has restored
peace to all of Europe and his daughter will wed King Philip
of Spain—the Catholics are smug as ever and raise their glasses,
while the Protestants scurry in shadow and fear—I close my
visor and mark the holy cross against my chest and the king
returns the gesture—I salute him and the audience roars and
I heft my shield with the golden lion painted 'cross it and my
horse runs his hoof through the dirt and I understand what
needs be done—the flag is dropped and we charge—I bring the
lance down late and, catching the king by his mask, it splinters
into a thousand pieces, and so he is undone—

I know this will be my undoing—I will be forced from this
land, but I will return like Jesus with my army, prepared to
beat this palace to dust and rebuild it within three days' time.

## Henry II, 40,
## Duc d'Orleans & King of France

My mare has ridden strong today and sweat froths on her hide and I lean into her neck and whisper, *This is your last run, mi amour,* and I stroke her mane that some servant has perfumed, the odor of lilacs and roses rises into my face, and I am a small child again in the royal garden tossing a red ball high in the air and catching it and rolling it down the lanes and running after it and catching it up again and darting through that labyrinth of hedges and fleeing from my nurses and guards until they could no longer find me and still I ducked through bushes and ran around great rock piles and fountains and statues of my king father and statues of my queen mother and I laughed to myself as they called my name and I ran into a clearing, a sight I'd never seen, hundreds of rosebushes all blooming reds and yellows and pinks and again I tossed my ball, red as the red roses, higher than ever, and as I watched it rise like a bleeding sun, I stumbled back into one of the bush's thorny arms and it caught me and bit my skin and burned and would not let me go—and no matter how loud I cried for my nurses and for my guards and for my king and for my queen no one came and I was bloodied and burning, alone—

I lower my golden visor and heft my lance and call, *Alle anon,* and we are off, galloping as if pulled by Dame Fortune herself, and my lance is level so that my shoulder burns and my captain's weapon takes me in the head and I lose my mount and mind, my horse no longer between my thighs, the perfume gone forever, and I am in utter whiteness and the weight of my armor holds me supine to the earth and for a wretched second I think to cry for my queen and to cry for my mistress but I am once more bloodied and burning, alone—

## Michel de Nostredame, 55,
## Physician & Seer, Astrologer & Occultist

Two months ago as I sat in the darkness of my room, well past midnight, a candle burned and the mandrake root burned and the call of an owl in the woods burned my ears—the folio was set before me on the hardwood table that a man made for me many years ago when I cured his child of plague, the same disease that, like a thief in the night, stole my wife and two babes—a strong wind blew through my open window and the candle bent and righted itself again and I dipped the old quill and waited for the vision to come, brief but fully realized before me—I witnessed that scene as surely as I see my good king now, grounded, and I wrote as I saw:

> The Lion shall overcome the old
> On the field of war in a single combat;
> He will pierce his eyes in a cage of gold
> This is the first of two lappings, then he dies a cruel death.

I know His Majesty surely will die of these wounds and that ten days hence, his loyal subjects will come to my home with pitchforks and strong rope and demand my life, and I know too that my patron, Queen Catherine, will protect me, her special seer—just as I know that Gabriel will be fled from Paris to Normandy and there gather a rebel army that will fail and he will be captured and, just before the axe kisses his neck, the executioner will bend to his ear and whisper that his wife and children will be removed from their lands and made to be beggars—I will continue to pen these prophecies, envisioning even my own death, because all I ever see, cruel necromancer

I am become, is darkness, death, and disease—where go the beauties and loves and lusts, the little graces and foibles by which to laugh? Still, I will see farther and farther into the future, five hundred years and more, and I know that in that far-off time, long after the ways of the Habsburgs and the Medicis and the House of Valois have passed into the ether, I will be remembered and studied and considered—perhaps that is all the beauty I need, and so I write of the twenty-first century:

> *The Son of Nazareth is no more,*
> *The Son of the Sun is no more,*
> *Yet the seer is seen by those who see,*
> *And the sun will drown the land with sea.*

# Old Hickory: Dickinson v. Jackson

*Stemming from a Welched Bet and a Challenge of Infidelity,*
*near Harrison's Mill on the Banks of the Red River,*
*Logan County, Kentucky,*
*a Full Day's Ride from Nashville, Tennessee,*
*May 30, 1806*

## Charles Dickinson, 26,
## Attorney & Winner of Twenty-Six Previous Duels

Governor Sevier has given me to understand I could
no longer postpone this interview—I spent the last
month on Mississippi riverboats practicing my pistol till
I could bury four shots in a row through the king card's
eye—this last week I woke each dawn howling in bed, begging Charlotte to cool the burning in my throat, the fire in
my heart—my stomach hollow as a chicken skull, my hands
so bloody a-tremble I could not even pen apologies if I'd
pleased—Sevier cajoled me to this purpose with a promise to
appoint me chief magistrate and so surpass my father's mere
assessment of me—his sneer forever wrapped 'round that
meerschaum pipe, the odor of his Cavendish tobacco linger-
ing in my clothes and hair, the incessant clicking of his teeth
on clay as he marked my legal opinions—where is he now, that
man who sent me to this wilderness, gone broke on his own
speculations, driven mad down to debtors' prison—where too
my father-in-law, whose horse came up lame and lost—my
thoughts run about heedless as a headless pullet—because of
my steady hand, I've been coaxed to wrangle this ruffian's
honor for months, yet now as I stand just twenty-four feet
from him—his hair a red tornado, his lipless mouth like an
axe mark hacked into rough-hewn wood, his wild gray eyes
themselves the color of lead, which say clear that he will be
king and not Sevier nor Jesus nor Satan himself can refute
his course—I can't steady the shake in my wrists, the pistol's
weight grown too great to handle—I can taste vomit on the
back of my tongue and my cheeks blanch and my breath

catches throatwise—I regret the black mark I've checked against his wife's good name and not because theirs is a lawful marriage—God knows it is not—rather, because that besmirch may have me meet the Elect before the next election ever comes.

On his man's word, I raise my arm and release my bullet first and it passes through his oversized coat and he does not flinch—a miss, by God!—now I know I am doomed—I suck in my gut and turn completely sideways but I stagger-swoon backward, dumbstruck—I would beg forgiveness if I thought it would soothe this scoundrel's soul—I hear his gun misfire, a mere tap like my father's teeth clicking clay, but this sound is the sweetest, loudest one I've ever known.

## Witness: Rachel Jackson, 39,
## Wife & Bigamist

Mister Jackson has lit out for Kentucky again, lit out on
horseback with friends again, *For business*, he said, but I
am no fool: I know where he goes and I know what he gains—
off to Philadelphia twice to be among the men who shape the
world because he, who has yet to put seed in my womb and I
imagine never will, has designs to lead this nation—he, who
cares more for the snort of a horse than that of a cognac—
Lord, I love him and I would defend him against an army of
detractors with either wit or whip—why then did I dream last
night that I followed him through the hardwood forests that
grow aside the Tennessee River, riding our prized Truxton
in the dew of the morning and sun-dappled noon—the azalea
bushes in full bloom with wisteria vines married through,
their long purple streams twining amid the pink plump tangles
and blaring white blossoms and little flutter-byes twittered by
and doves cooed their coos and where he stopped to water his
horse the river kept its course, straight and true, when from
the water a beast arose and came streaming ashore to stand
before him and unfasten its fur which fell from its body as if it
were robes to pool in the earth like the black fur rug that lies
on our parlor floor and there standing before my husband, a
naked Cherokee squaw—her eyes like almonds and honey, her
hair a brunette river run over the cliffs of her shoulders—his
hands go to her and the sun drops like a seed cone and darkness attends them and I watch now from my vantage high in
an old hickory as they couple on the floor of the woods crying
each other's secret names and I weep and watch by light of full

moon, which shines on me, and they discover me there, weeping and swooning and naked, watching and watched.

Now I pine away the morning, sitting on the stone steps looking over the planted estate where everything grows verdant and ripens. Our slaves go about picking fruits and hoeing earth, and one of them, Long Feather, is in the stable and his fine form, I think, comes from his mix of Creek and African blood. He will come to the out-kitchen soon for his lunch bucket of molasses and biscuit and ham, and Long Feather, whose hair is black as Truxton's mane, will wear an odor of horse froth and oats, and he'll lead Truxton to the back door and he'll be saddled and Long Feather will lift me up and oh how I shall ride him.

## Andrew Jackson, 39,
## Ex-Senator, Judge, Major General,
## & Son of Scots Irish Immigrants

I swear on my mother's sweet soul I will blow him through,
as certain as he has blown on my embers till the flames
grew into an all-consuming fire that shall lay waste to any challenge before me, or any base fool like this poltroon here who
uttered the vile calumny against my dear Rachel, a fierce buck-
ing beauty herself—she can ride Truxton through town without
even wearing her gloves, and if a man so much as speak her
name I will tie him to the first tree, let alone one so base as to
claim I'd made bigamy with her—I should have pistol-whipped
this puppy when he first began his rumor-seeding but I knew
him to be but a lickspittle in some other man's fight—still, he
is of British birth and so a born bastard and this Dickinson
shall receive no less than what I have promised Mother to visit
upon every man Jack soldier of that son of a whore, England,
whose brutes killed both my brothers—one by bullet and one by
exposure in a Carolina prison camp where they cut my cheek
and poisoned Robert with vile tack slathered in rat grease—they
drove sweet Mother to her early grave too—what I'd not give to
see that woman again, to have her ease my burning brow with
her cool hands and gray eyes, those bottomless pools of affec-
tion so alike to Rachel's—I'd even let this rascal live so he could
admire the morning fog as it settles among the pine needles—
but that cannot be—there is only this one life, this one chance
to alter the shape of the world, before we enter the eternal
damnation of silence and utter darkness and she died in my

arms blessing the vengeance I swore on every lobsterback son of a bitch I could bury.

The judge calls fire and before I can even aim, his ball cuts through my ribs and I hear the damn things break—I am dead, by God—I mash my mouth into a razor line, wheeze through my nose, and the sweat bursts in my eyes, near blinding me—I level the pistol and squeeze the trigger but the gun only half fires—my chin starts to tremble when the smell of Mother's laundry lye overwhelms me and Rachel's breath is on my neck and her hand comes over mine and steadies the gun and we re-cock the hammer together and pull the trigger and send our shot into his piss-proud belly and he shuffles back and flops to the ground, legs all aflail, and he has surely spent his last day on earth and my blood runs down my body but I am alive, and because I am, so too is Mother, and Rachel besides, and we shall so remain until we all enter oblivion together.

# Man above Challenge: Dauphin v. Culver

*A First–Blood Duel with Colichemardes,*
*behind the St. Louis Cathedral, New Orleans, Louisiana,*
*April 3, 1834*

Speaker: *Tim-tim!*

Audience: *Bois sec.*

Speaker: *Cassez-li . . .*

Speaker and Audience together: *. . . dans tchu* (bonda) *macaque.*

       —Traditional Creole Call to Story, from Lafcadio Hearn's
               *Gombo Zhèbes: Little Dictionary of Creole Proverbs*

## Emile Dauphin, 19,
## French Creole

He should not have crossed Canal and into our Quarter, nor entered the octoroon ball and defiled it with his odious taint, like too much choupique at the Bienville Market. These Kaintock keelboat rats have done much to damage our town—set fire to the Tchoupitoulas Street Fair where Papa kept his cattle and killed Monsieur Gaetano's dancing bear in his Congo Square circus. He is indeed beneath my birth, yet I feel the need to lash and strike this boorish tramp who approached sweet Yvonne, whose sister I keep in a clean white cottage on Rue Rampart, and pulled her hand from Jean Philip's and barked back the timid boy, affrighted I suppose by stories of Wild Bill Sedley and other riverboat bullies. He would not heed my call so I demanded his blood from my blow, or he could have mine in turn, and though his shoulders are thick as any field Negro's, I possess the skills—two full seasons under the tutelage of Garland Croquere, my *maitres d'armes*, the swiftest mulatto you ever saw, but whom I have surely outgrown, and he will see so in my stance and in the grace with which I dispatch this ruffian—tomorrow *mes amis* in cafes will sing how deftly I did defeat our enemy.

We cross on cypress boards laid in the pitch mud, two Negroes before us with lighted flambeaux to see our way to St. Anthony's Park, hidden from sight by the bustling gowns of Spanish moss, and I recall when I was but fourteen and walking this very banquette, a Kaintock and I came to an impasse until our eyes met and I acquiesced and stepped down into the muck, and though I was loath to look back, when

I did I saw that Papa had moved off as well—I wish he could see me now as I strike this oaf and his blood runs down his lips and onto his filthy fingertips, the ones he rubbed on sweet Yvonne's thin wrists and she did not even flinch at his gaucherie, but now I have my honor and I will retrieve her as my own reward—Jean Philip be damned.

## Dale Culver, 23,
## Riverboat Kaintock

I seen this purty half-breed gal, covered in cream-colored
lace, dancing with some princey French fool and so stiffened my back paddleboard straight and said, *Scuse me now, son,*
*but I'm cutting on in,* but I really wanted to knock hell out that sissy
and flang that gal over my shoulder like a fifty-pound sack of
sugar and skidaddle with her back to the keelboat and if I had
to fight off the boys who'd try to make sport of her, well I'd
holler em back with my fists and the trusty blade I keep in my
boot, shouting, *I'm a man made of anvil and alligator, been weaned on wolf*
*milk and whiskey; got dynamite for a heart and snake spit for blood; any man*
*what touch my gal will count himself lucky not to wake with his ears missing or an*
*eye gouged out or his tongue torn from his flappy jaw,* when this other little
dandy here pokes me in the chest and says he's her escort—he
is, him—what goes the size of a bantam pullet I've lost money
on, and me with red turkey feather in cap to show I'm the
bully of my boat, been hauling on a cordelle and pulling the
sweeps since I was twelve, so I laughed in his face but he just up
and took my nose between his knuckles and twisted and ever
last one of them Frenchies stepped back and even the musicians stopped they song, and buddy boy, I knew the score—but
before I could call, *Put up your dukes,* he says to me, *Sir, let us as*
*gentlemen satisfy our honor,* but I have absolute no use for this dumb
show of dignity—what good is your honor, man, when you are
dead and in the grave?

Yet here I am, tightening my grip till my knuckles burn
white 'round the handle of this wooden sword, blood pounding in my barking-mad mind, and I surge to strike and bash

this boy's head but the Nongela rye's got me bandy-leg'd as the first time I ever took to a boat, so I rise and swing and stumble again, and he taps my noggin and splits my bottom lip clean in two like a pig's hoof and he says, *It is done; let us repair*, and turns his back to me but I am not done: I slip out the sweet steel I've carried all the way from Louisville to fend off pirates and bushwhackers—you wanted some of my blood, boy, but I will take all of yours.

## Garland Croquere, 59,
*Maitres d'armes*, Mulatto, FMC

Standing in the mud of the street, I study the grease
tracks from rats' backs smeared along the foundations
of this city's homes, when Emile and his coterie pour out the
Orleans Theatre, where I am barred because of the brown in
my skin—though I am lighter than the proud mothers who
auction their daughters in there—I knew a challenge had been
made, knew in my heart it was Emile's own doing because he is
rash and he is foolish—why his mother has paid me to protect
his life—it is too late for me to intercede, the weapons and
site already agreed upon while I was out here, ankle-deep in the
stinking sludge of the street that the blacks have named Croquere
in my honor, the same dignity bestowed me by the whites in
Paris, where I would escort every color of woman known in
this world and we went anywhere we chose and I killed four
whites in duels and an Algerian too and the people and papers
begged me to stay but I came home to this city where no white
will honor me even with barrel or blade—instead I must stand
near wooden gutters that smell of garbage and night soil, yet
if Emile loses this fight, as his teacher, I too am insulted but
without means of redress.

My pulse slows as Emile draws first blood from the brute,
and heedless to our rules, the Kaintock presses his lip to his
shoulder and curses and crouches and takes up a bowie knife,
and though I am, as second, expected to aid my man, I hesi-
tate and let him draw the blade across Emile's thin neck and
the tiniest wound smiles there, then yawns, and the blood

breaks black down his shirtfront and Emile falls, gagging and dying, yet my heart springs full and my fingertips tingle as I draw my rapier and prepare to run this white man through and what true soul among us would dare question my rights now.

# Pistols at Twenty Paces: Lacroix v. Thigpen

*On the Last Recorded Duel in Hancock County, Mississippi,
April 23, 1866*

## Philip Lacroix, 51,
## Colonel, CSA

He robbed me more grossly than Grant, more deeply than
Lincoln, and these twenty paces pale compared to the
one thousand miles and more I walked from that captured
officers' camp in Illinois where snow seeped through shoe soles
so cold I cut felt from my hat to patch them warm and dry and
back home the courthouse burned down—damn that Gen'ral
Butler, I'd hang him were I the governor—and with it went
all the county records—deeds and land titles and all—my slaves
were freed and stole what all they could carry and after I'd taken
such good care of them as God set forth for me in dominion,
so this traitor and coward and former friend, who ate of my
lunch Sundays after church, could take my lawful owned cattle
and claim them for his own, after I branded their hides while
my darkies held them still. The smell of torched flesh in my hair
and nose, that odor so like a battlefield, while a persistent wind,
like this one, blows brittle leaves and cools the sweat burning on
my skin and the judge hollers, *Fire.*

I turn and squeeze the stiff trigger—I know I am right in
this course and God will prove me true with the aim of my
bullet: hot sulfur smell, thick smoke in sunlight, and a snarl
of flame like the hell we're both bound for.

## Etiene Thigpen, 46,
## Veteran, US Artillery Division

He come home a fool-headed war hero to judge and insult me—we walked down to the lower field of fresh-turned earth—iron and onion and scat—where he accused me of stealing his cows which I had bought clear, got a cash ticket for proof, and now I'm sorry I ever prayed for his sorry-ass soul—sure I ran some hooch out to the blockade, but that don't make me no damn traitor, just a trader with them boys in blue who gave me coffee—the same chic'ry then as what coats my tongue now—and more, I suffered the hardships of war, boiling seawater to get at the salt to keep my food, and done fought my war too—took a bullet in Mexico with Robert E. Lee and now my sweat-clammy palms wrap 'round this pistol butt, smell horse lather and oil on this iron piece, see them mildewed Spanish moss tendrils come ribboning off oaks slashed by sunbeams—accuse me of stealing and lying to boot, I refute his claim same as I did old Thibideaux's back in '53, may God rest his soul in smoke and flame eternal, *Fire.*

I turn and my hand blooms a white cloud of smoke as though I'm holding a fistful of baby's breath: good gracious, boys, I'm hit and done; please say sweet things of me to Mary.

## Mrs. Etiene Thigpen
## (née Mary Annette Cuevas), 18,
## Watching Her Husband Duel

From where I crouch behind the pleached crosshatching
of azalea branches, I see the two men standing back to
back like stuck twins and wonder how they can be that close
and not kill each other now—Etiene's face flushed, his shoes,
as always, thick with mud, and that preening blowhard, Philip,
just as calm as Sunday afternoon, his clothes pressed and his
boots polished and shined, prepared for death or murder one,
yet it's my hands that rattle these petals from the branches—
beyond them the gulf catches the sunlight in little spinning
coins, like the bright dimples in the cheeks of the Kaintock
man who touched my wrist at the Saint Stanislaus social and
who, in that moment, bade me run away with him to New
Orleans—to stroll along the banquettes arm in arm under the
ironworked balconies and to eat almond truffles or pralines
brought 'round by Creole women wearing bright-colored
tignons and hoop earrings that brush their bare shoulders like
I wish I could wear mine—we'd attend the Conde Street balls,
dancing and sweating under the flambeaux, where we'd glide
through the measures of the contredanse or sip wine in the
American cabarets until I'd retire to his arms and bed and
he could take my ankles and toes in his mouth and I'd take
him in mine and he'd not smell like cattle and night soil—I
yearn to leave this backwood outhouse, these backward outhouse men, whose petty wars and self-puffery leave me hungry
as the war ever did, when I had to parch corn to make coffee

till my guts were pulled like the dead girl from my womb, whom I buried in secret while Etiene was off making whiskey or God knows what, to walk away as these men here have walked away, one from the other, but without sense enough between them to know it better to continue to walk and never to turn around as they have turned now—*Fire*.

A twin roaring, two great clouds of smoke, and a scream— I have prayed for this bittersweet moment—the taking of Etiene away from me—in my dreams I am not his little Mary Annette, hiding behind a bush, heart pounding so hard it makes my hands shake, but rather, I am the bullet squeezed from the burning steady barrel, freed.

# Check, Mate: Johnson v. Rasputin

*Nine Months after Johnson Was Sentenced to Prison*
*for Breaking the 1910 Mann Act for a Crime*
*He Allegedly Committed in 1909,*
*Staying in a Royal Apartment, St. Petersburg, Russia,*
*March 3, 1914*

## Arthur John (Jack) Johnson, 35,
## World Heavyweight Boxing Champion
## & Fugitive from "American Justice"

Pop put his belt to my back regular as the mindless
and violent Galveston weather that spun his birds
about in the sun and in the rain, and he would come again,
a hurricane of a man, to hit me in the head with a skillet so's
I couldn't run a comb through my hair for a week, or he'd
swing his jump rope that whipped the wind just as it cracked
against my skin, random as The Numbers, till that summer
morn when I brought Mama's red clay pitcher filled with water
to the rooftop and there I set it on the stoop and removed one
by one his trained pigeons from their coop and dunked them,
beak-down, till their wings quit batting my forearms and their
last living breath bubbled up and popped into thin air and
was gone forever and then I set them out on a sideboard like
in these pheasant still-life paintings hung against the velvet
walls in this well-appointed room, just so I'd know the exact
minute of my next beating—and it was my last one, too—as soon as
I could stand again I left home and fought my way through the
world and beat black men in makeshift rings or barbershops,
but the first time I fought a white man, the cops threw us both
in the clink with nothing to do but spar, two pugilists training
for ninety straight no-women days, and he taught me to give
it as well as to take and when I got out I swore I'd never spend
another dime of my time in a place like that and I got out and
put the whipping on blacks and whites alike, though truthfully,
they were all just Pop to me.

Rasputin takes my queen so I, according to the rules we've invented, take another shot of potato vodka—twelve so far this game, our second one of the night—I stand to hit the head and go all wobbly, spin, and kick the board over, and the game is undone, pieces clink and shoot across the marble floor and I too hit the floor, cool and hard, and laugh, realizing for the first time in a decade or more, I have been knocked slap out.

## Gregori Rasputin, 42,
## Mystic Religious Leader & Advisor to the Romanovs

Here is God's own hand at beauty, this mystical black man in fur coat and Buddha cheek, full of grace and fury and quick of wit and smile, but he cannot drink to save his life let alone his race or country, and there on the chaise longue reclines his whore-wife, who takes each shot like the Lord's own body, and my Ekaterina strokes her hair and they purr together there and it remains unspoken between us men that the winner shall take all—this fighter, so used to having his way with every man he battles and every woman he woos, which is just another kind of battle, has left his lady open and I slide my bishop, cocked at an angle, right up her side and pull her to my lip of the board and I pour his shot rim-high and he holds it like a prayer bead, steady as winter hail, and throws it down and blows out his spirit and shakes his head and topples—his deep eyes roll back in his head like those of my epileptic sister Maria as she floundered in the Tura River below our Siberian home, not a bird above nor a fish below but snow and snow and cold cold snow—when they pulled her out her lips were the Prussian blue of cyanide—like those of my brother Dmitri, who with me fell into that same river and only I escaped to live and thrive—now in the Russian winter the pale air that twists from my lips is but their spinning bodies come to invade me no matter how I've tried to snuff them out.

I have always lived by this one creed: the greater the sin, the greater the redemption. It's why I explained the pointlessness of flagellation to the Khlysty—if you are to deny the body, brother, why excite the senses with pain when there is so much pleasure to be had—now beside his sleeping, snoring body I will have my way with his whore-wife and as I twist the long strands of my chin whiskers and pull them taut, the Lord begins to excite and shake my crystal bones, move through me, and make my tongue the trumpet of His good grace with which to sing a gospel into the great chasm of these very Mothers of God.

## Lucille Cameron, 21,
## Prostitute, Secretary, & Wife to Jack Johnson

After that bitch lied on the stand, Jack skipped bail
and we fled to a Mexican town where we could hear
the church bells tolling all the way down to the beach where
Jack and I, hand in hand, followed the mule tracks in the dry
sand, the wind erasing them one grain at a time. We passed
fishermen in wooden dinghies, which bobbed in the water
like coffins; passed kids who flew kites made of yesterday's
newspapers; turned off at Calle Vida and entered the town's
only cemetery, where we joined the old women who wore
pressed and austere gowns, white with embroidered roses and
tangles of thorny stems. They swept dirt and salt off their
loved ones' crypts and put fresh-cut flowers and candles on
top of brightly painted tombs—pinks and pale oranges, light
blues and greens—like muted versions of the hump houses in
our Paris on the Prairie. I pulled away and walked back among
the poorest graves, some nothing more than ash in a mason jar
or a lone crucifix stabbed into the earth. And then this one:
a small pair of faded blue pants and a red and blue striped
shirt, both folded sharp as surgical tools, held in place against
the blowing wind by an ash-filled plastic bag, and like a lamb-
skin condom, it had burst where a bone that didn't quite burn
had pushed through. I put my fingertip to it, pushed it back
as gentle as you please, and brushed away the leaves and said
a prayer to Mary for this dead child and for mine too, who'd
be about size enough now to wear these clothes.

Now sitting on this velour chair beneath crystal chan-
deliers that hang twenty feet above, I tamp the tears down,

because I know there's no going back to Mexico, nor to the United States, nor to a time before that law was passed, before they needed a Great White Hope and found it only in the form of Uncle Sam; back before the operation or before my innocence was stolen by Uncle Ray's wandering hands—there's no back at all and there's certainly no tomorrow—there is only the giving in to the moment—Ekaterina's hand on my thigh, her lips and breath on my neck, the moan caught in my throat, and this bright-eyed mystic standing before me, worshipful and tugging his beard. My man is the king—he has scraped through this life by way of nimble violence, though he appreciates delicate things—my thin wrists, the tsar's Fabergé eggs—the sheen of a simple pigeon feather can bring him to tears but this night is not his night: it will see no rise from him at all.

# Me and the Devil Blues: Johnson v. Trussle

*In a Cutting–Heads Contest near Itta Bena, Mississippi,*
*August 13, 1938*

## Robert Johnson, 27,
## Author of Twenty-Nine Published Songs

Now I'm back in the Delta having fun and folly with the old fool, Charlie—sure I ran his name through some mud but just to bend his bones a bit—he got raw about it, pointed that fret-pressin' knife at me, a simple threat from a simple gimp, and spoke up strong and stout and called me out to run guitars, ring notes from their necks, and I laughed and did a double take, couldn't hardly believe my ears let alone my eyes 'cause they been bad since the day I's born—reckon why I couldn't recognize that white man for what he was, standing there at the crossroads where the low moon made a shade of him, like some beast in black clothes—he got me to hit the road, head out west to San Antone, where I stood in a studio facing peeling wallpaper and singing so soft they made me record each tune twice—I put my soul in them songs and he sold them by the thousands till they turned into tiny coffins holding dead tracks—when I play some roadhouse show people always beg I do exact as on that wax, you know, like I's a jukebox built just for they pleasing, but to me that's just a prison, and I am dead set against repeating myself like that damn clock ticking on the grade school wall above the picture of a lynched god, white as white cotton ever got, where I spent my days studyin' how to jump a freight, didn't wait to get put behind no mule, hoeing up a row just to plod on back, so I quit that school and I quit this land and hobo'd a train north to Chicago, where I slept in cemeteries and sat on tombstones playing long enough that my fingers grew calluses so leather-thick I could grab a coal so quick out the fire and light my cig before I'd even begin to feel its warmth—still I can't shake the eerie notion that my life's passing before my ears and eyes—but if I'm hell bound, Mama, I'm ready to go; let the devil's hounds howl for me through the night.

So play your best, Chuck, then step aside, 'cause I'm gonna cut you so swift and deep, you'll spend the rest of your crippled life jaw-jacking 'bout how in this hell-hot weather you had your head severed by the damnedest bluesman ever.

## Charlie "Trickle Creek" Trussle, 67, Paraplegic & Unrecorded Slide Guitarist (Dedicated to Cedell Davis)

S ay he done sold his soul to the devil but what could a whelp like this boy h'yer ever know about the real hell I been through, though I know good and goddamn well I ain't got a snowball's chance to beat him—his fingers nimble as spiders on a web, perfect as a pocket watch tick—still, what I'm supposed to do, take raw guff off this bragging rogue, let him disrespect me, call me Cripple Creek, as if having polio and being wheelchair-bound makes me less a man than him? Ain't I throbbing with the same desire as any other body? But boy if my hands could bloom, flower like a fetus in womb, I'd make the tunes I hear in my head and shame this cur, smiling in pinstripes and plucking away. Instead, I scraped out bar chords and bullied short runs with this butter knife I stole from St. Anne's Orphanage. And when he sings, *Hello, Satan, I believe it's time to go*, I look down at the devil's own doing: my claws; my fists curled tight into palsied balls, tight as when I'd crawl drunk into Lila's lap as we lay in my cot out back of Manning's Auto Repair, way back before she left on that Greyhound searching for someone to fill her with that baby she wanted; these same busted hands that could never hold still her steady rolling self, never mind the children we could not make.

In a flash I bust through my impotent rage and ram this blade through Bob's thick skull, but then I'm sober and awake again, sitting hangdog and silent, listening at him strum and pick and sing so goddamn beautiful it makes me want to cry.

## Lonnie Newhouse, 57,
## Witness, Owner of the Crossroads Saloon,
## & Cuckold

Hush up and listen at him, will ya: *I don't care where you bury my body, baby, once I'm good and gone.* This fool don't know half the truth he sings yet I'm more the fool for bringing my old lady 'round him in the first place—I should have reckoned that look in ole Bob's eyes the same as I give to them ole country gals—big thighs and jelly rolls—give em my rock and stroll home to sweet Irene—bathe till I'm fresh from beer and smoke and pleasure and flop beside her in our bed, where once I heard her call his name as she slept, though it sounded like his voice—thin and eerie as ghost speak—as if some wanting haint from another world was tasting on her tongue the name of its lover—at first I was spooked but then I grew howling mad as when Lou's ole blue tick got in my coop and ate the day's eggs, crushed them and licked they runny middle, which got me hot, sure as shit, but when I stepped into the light of day and seen the dead hens too, one after another littered on the yard, all twisted in bloody heaps, and knew he'd killed them just for fun—well, man, I went buck wild and straight off to the Dreyfus Druggerie and got me some strychnine and stuffed it into a chunk of raw meat and it was a pure de-light to watch that mangy dog suffer, moaning and whimpering three days into death—last night old Roustabout Tommy told me how this singing mutt here slicked my gal and tangled her hair good and I pictured them twinning and hanking on the bed where our baby was born and I began to howl and to plot—tonight I'm gonna do this boy in with a hot spiked drink of gin and then he too has got to go, I guarantee.

# Custody Battle for Chelsea Tammy:
## Malgrove v. Bowling

*At the Toys "R" Us, Aisle 6, in Minneapolis, Minnesota,*
*December 24, 1983 (for Jeanne Leiby)*

# Tyler Malgrove, 38,
## Attorney & Divorced Father
## of a Six-Year-Old Daughter

I am a trial attorney. I make a damn respectable living through confrontation. I own a Saab turbo sedan, a closet full of Polo and Armani, and a Movado watch my wife gave me on our fifth anniversary. I bought a three-bedroom ranch and my Jennifer attends the finest prep school and my wife drives the Volvo 240 that I paid for in cash and lost along with the house when she divorced me last year. She was a cheerleader, my wife, at the University of Georgia, and her legs are long and golden. She is great at parties, her platinum feathered hair tousles when she laughs, and when she laughs, you are the only man in the world. And whom does she laugh for now? When she leaves a conversation, she'll touch your wrist with her long bronze fingers and you go deaf for the next four minutes. And because our daughter's play pals all have this doll, she must have one too. The hell with the forty dollars; I want her to be supernormal and I want my old life back. So I slipped inside my Lucchese boots and drove to five different stores before I arrived here to find the last doll left on the bottom shelf and so I reach for little—what's her name?—Chelsea Tammy, with her red yarn hair and dimples, when some guy decked out like Rambo in fatigues and dog tags and lank hair tries to take her from me. I say, *Sir, I believe you'd be more fit for Raggedy Andy.* My kid may not have her father now but she'll damn sure have whatever else she wants—when he reaches for my tie, I slap his hand away.

Buddy boy, I did not grow up picking cotton in northern

Alabama, did not join the National Guard to pay my way
through undergrad and law school at UGA, did not woo a
woman as beautiful as all the gold in Fort Knox, did not join
the bar to gain a foothold in society and earn the respect of
men better than your vagrant self will ever be, and certainly
did not suffer through a very messy and very public divorce,
which left me bankrupt of money and wife and child, just to
lose what my baby girl wants now. Not to you. Not to anyone.
I say, *Unhand me, sir*, and then, as his grip tightens around my
throat, I squeal, *Or I'll sue! I'll sue!*

## Sam Bowling (a.k.a. "Pin"), 31, Vietnam Veteran & Divorced Father of an Eight-Year-Old Daughter

I yank him to me and grab hold of his neck right below his bobbin apple and squeeze and it feels good and I am back on R and R in the Thanh Hotel, downtown Saigon, '72, and Chi will be my girlfriend for the week and she feeds me shrimp dumplings dipped in fish sauce and I drink cold beer in a glass and she rubs lemongrass oil into my feet and palms and massages my manhood until it blooms and bursts and she takes me to a deep hot bath, my first in months, and then to a sauna and I am limp and the air is full of vanilla and walnut and in here there is no smell of decay nor earthen rot that seeps into your pores and will not wash out with Lux soap and a trickle shower and she brings me to a bedroom where I lie on fresh linens and incense burns in a little clay pot and I inhale the vapor of opium and follow the lazy whir of a ceiling fan until my eyes grow heavy and I fall into a sleep—a far war's cry from my rucksack in a fresh-dug ditch when I'm out in the bush, and I dream of childhood Christmas with luminaries down our snow-dappled driveway and waking up to the rich smells of bacon and biscuits and coffee percolating on the stove top and my mother in an apron and my father at the table reading the *Herald* in his black socks and there is only one present under the tree and it is for me and I crawl underneath and reach and open it and a rat lunges at me—I awake in Vietnam and I sit up and see the red stains on the white sheets about me and they are the color of old blood and I know I am killed and I scream, and lying next to me is Chi, my assassin,

and she screams too until I wrap my hands around her neck,
the white gold of my wedding band bright against her dark skin
and the veins in her temple stand out and I remember crawl-
ing in one of the Cu Chi tunnels expecting to find a punji stake-
pit but instead finding some dink bastard who had me dead to
rights with his pistol and he pulled the trigger but nothing
happened and I grabbed him by the throat—didn't even shoot
him, just squeezed the life from him—even when I realize the
blood is just the red clay come leached from my open pores, I
keep right on squeezing her—

Just as I do this yuppie bastard here: one hand on his
throat and one on the box with the doll inside and what can
they do to stop me from killing him as dead as all the others
I've buried in my brain?

## Chuck Simpson, 19,
## Stock Boy & Drug Dealer

I came from hiding another stupid fat-face doll out back
behind the Dumpster—that makes seventeen total, and at
forty bucks a pop, that equals . . . shit if I know, like a thousand bones, I guess, way more than I make at this job or ped-
dling dime bags to my sister's pals, though Megan looks long
at me when I give her the shotgun and our lips damn near
brush—I've carried a crush on her for years and will make my
move when she starts high school next fall—back inside under
the fluorescent lights I hate myself for humming along with
"Karma Chameleon" for like the tenth time today and I walk
down aisle eleven past little baskets of cinnamon candles to
see Jimmy, the boss, yelling and waving all crazy—he's been
side-eyeing me all week and I guess he's caught on to my trick
and now the jig is up, as they say in the movies—he'll fire me
on Christmas Eve of all dang days and what will I tell Mom as
we sip the brandy with apple cider she simmers in the Crock-
Pot and smoke our cigs on the front porch and wonder again
what happened to Pops and where he's gone but we won't say
nothing as we slurp hooch from our coffee mugs until we're
tight—dang, man, that's just paranoid pot talk—I turn the corner on aisle six, pig-eyed and slow, and there's Jimmy deep
in a melee like the bad guy who jumps in a match to help Ric
Flair beat Dusty Rhodes—and I run past Trivial Pursuit and
Monopoly displays, stunned that this is my life—two dudes on
the linoleum wrestling over a toy and Jimmy in the middle
of it—the one dude looks like my dealer and the other is a
dweeby hotshot, the kind who acts like he owns the world and

is about to start charging me rent, but Jimmy is my dweeb and I'd like to clean his clock, but he's got his knee in this dude's back like the cops did me junior year in the school parking lot as I was rolling a lousy doobie and now I know Jimmy's not my manager at all—he's a narc, and that's for dang sure.

I ease around the scuffle and pick up the doll they've dropped and head to the back to gather my thousand dollars in the Dumpster and Jimmy can't fire me now 'cause I quit—Zeppelin's on my car stereo and I'm already at Aladdin's Castle playing Joust or Dragon's Lair, high and happy these holidays, and it's gonna be a good Christmas, Mom, because even though I'm a dropout, I ain't no dummy after all.

# The Magic Hour: Garriga v. Garriga

*Inside a Pool Set on the Living Room Floor and, Later,
in the Tallahassee Memorial Hospital,
Tallahassee, Florida,
June 26–27, 2011*

## Megan Garriga, 32,
## Laboring Mother-to-Be

**M**idwife said, *Reach up and feel his head.* He should be here by now, been dilated nine centimeters for more than ten hours and I've paced and squatted and showered, bathed, puked, and danced with Michael and rocked on the ball while breathing breathing breathing—*It's hard work, it hurts like hell, and I can do this, it's hard work, it hurts like hell, and I can do this*—he should be in my arms already yet I'm still surprised when my fingertips go inside and trace the wet curve of the not-yet-crowning scalp—he's there, he's really there, and I feel triumphant, strong for the next wave, so I lean back in this pool of water, my arms and legs straight out, floating, my feet spongy and fish white and wrinkled and I am weightless—a storm is blowing outside and I want to fall asleep but my body begins to flex again and I rise to meet it, squat and set myself ready for the work—I lean over the round edge of the vinyl tub and I am naked in front of people I barely know, modesty a luxury that passed hours ago, and now I lock eyes and hands with Michael, his voice smooth as he tells me that he was born in a storm just like this one and I am seized suddenly and want to crawl out of my body—why won't he crawl out of mine?—Michael's voice calls me back from the edge, sounding the same as it did years ago when we lived seven hundred miles apart and he wooed me over the phone for hours at a time and I fell in love with him over those wires, stretched bellying between poles, and as long as his voice stays strong and calm I know everything will be all right and I can't even imagine my baby's face, only the feeling of holding him, dense and small and warm against me—I bend my hand into the imagined curve of his tiny butt, his ghost legs curled into my chest—and I look up to find Michael's eyes and I find them and I want to give him our son in this rainstorm, and I breathe out, the wave receding, and try not to throw up as I burp twice in a row for the millionth time today and the rain keeps pounding the porch's tin roof and I reach inside again to feel his head but he hasn't moved a bit, still a full finger's reach away.

# Michael Garriga, 39,
## Father-to-Be

Megan's labored now for more than a day, insanely drug-free, and our heads are pressed together and my arms drape her and we both moan through the pain—hers unknowable to me and mine a mere helplessness—I have manned the stove top all day to keep the pool water warm and it is dusk out and rain bangs the windows and we are in a lull now and Megan's half asleep and I say, *I was born during a storm like this*, which is an absolute lie, but I don't know what else to do—I want her pain to ease and it seems like the thing to say and she is naked in the pool on the verge of another contraction, they're coming one on top of the other now, and earlier I feared she'd lose control in the shower, in the tub, on the bed, on the ball, but she never did though I am on that scattered horizon myself, and I have fed her frozen grapes and Gatorade and coconut Popsicles and the leaves are turning in the wind, their underbellies prone, and she's pushing again and I moan with her and the windows are streaked with dirt and rain, which run down in a slurry, and stalks and sheets of lightning brighten the sky and she's draped over the edge of the pool, her breath slowing, and she is pale and glazy-eyed—a great thunder shakes the house and the sky goes bright and the candles all flicker in their stands, *What if she's electrocuted?* and I hold her against my chest and the midwife, lounging on the couch, says, *Y'all are doing great*, and I want a bourbon so bad and it's right there in that cabinet but what will the midwife think, what will Megan?

Another wave is on her and we're breathing again, and

what if, once here, the baby learns what a selfish child I am or, worse yet, what if he rightly hates me—what if, after all of this agony and planning, he's stillborn, has Down's, is deaf? How will I deal with that? As this fear washes over me, Megan grabs my wrists and I roll my forehead against hers, *Breathe, baby, just breathe and stay in this moment.*

## Baby Boy, Several Hours Later,
## Tallahassee Memorial Hospital

In an instant all will vanish and we'll be alone once more, in
the midst of nothingness. I will cause breath to enter you and
ye shall live.

*— Waiting for Godot* and Ezekiel 37:5

W e have always been alone in this dark wet world,
floating, but then a strong force urges us toward the
light and our head's crimped against something bone hard and
hurting and the rhythm of our life—the old *bum-hum hum-hum*—
has lately gone wild like *bumbumbumbumbumbum*, and just now
we've gone numb and distant moans have grown loud and ter-
rifying, something beyond the great void calling us, insistent,
irresistible, and there are convulsions all about us and pierc-
ing beeps and loud voices drown out our rhythm, our beat is
gone, and we are lifeless when a suction grabs our skull and we
feel like we'll be ripped inside out and the flesh tears about us
and we head into the light, water spilling over our skin, and
I am separated from we and I burn in light and my body is
so heavy my lungs will collapse and something sucks my nose
and lungs and I am screaming to drown out the deafening
noise about me, my eardrums set to burst, my lungs will im-
plode and the light sears my eyes even as I shut them, a red red
burning through, and I am dying, no doubt, I am dead and I
scream, *Help, help, help!* but who is there to hear—then I smell
a sweetness, a rich odor, and open my eyes and all is blurry
and there's a hazy angel before me, wings of the whitest gauze
spread before me and the smell is intense and I go to her and

open my mouth to say something, anything—her skin is warm on my freezing skin and there's our old heartbeat again—*bum-bum bum-bum*—and the wings fold about me, enshroud me, and I open and close my mouth, hungry to live, and that smell overtakes me and calms me, the sounds have receded to one soothing *shhhhh* and my mouth wraps around a nipple and all is quiet again, warm and safe with us, in this motherly heaven.

# Occupational Hazard or *Ars Poetica*:
## Shoulder Angel v. Shoulder Demon

*The Last Temptation of the Author,*
*Right Here, Right Now*

So I'll meet you at the bottom if there really is one / they always told me when you hit it you'll know it / but I've been falling so long it's like gravity's gone and I'm just floating.

— Drive-By Truckers

# Angel, Left Shoulder

He keeps muttering, *Without regret I'd have no memory at all, without regret I'd have no memory at all,* and I see an opening to save his soul, lace my fingers and unhinge my wings, inch up to my tippy toes on his shoulder bones, shut my eyes and lean soft into his ear: *Remember the bad health and poor choices, the broken van you could never really fix and the depth of that ditch; remember when you head-butted that stop sign and how your scalp bled and itched for weeks on end; remember crashing from your back door and pitching face-first into the rocks, the blood down your shirtfront and your neighbors, smoking dope on their back porch, chuckling at you; remember sleeping with your best friend's girl and how you've never forgiven yourself for his suicide—the concussions, the arrests, the near arrests, the times you should have been arrested so the police could have put a stop to you; remember getting caught when you shoplifted a candy bar even though you had a pocket full of cash and when you were arrested for DUI on a Friday night and couldn't make bail till Tuesday late because of MLK's holiday and you cursed that great man for his honor; remember the affairs, the near affairs, and the times you should have just fucked off; remember that four-day binge in which you drank only rye and woke up screaming from dehydration, and in the mirror by moonlight, you saw your skin puckered and wrinkled like some ancient ghoul, your fingers seized into knots—and if that wasn't rock bottom, then tell me what is—but you just added water with your bourbon next day and said,* Lesson learned; *remember the baby you had aborted and, afterward, the dream you had of that baby, the little girl who lacked bones in her thumbs but she was still just so beautiful; and remember weeping, apologizing to a picture of your own self as a baby,* You had so much potential, kid, *and now you have your own living baby and will you ever stop apologizing for that*—I feel his shoulder tense, muscles hunched like a bull's hump, and my halo dims and the light fades from my robes but then:

*You are loved by God and you are loved by me.* Nothing. *Your wife loves you, your family loves you, your mom, your friends, and your baby boy too.* Not a thing. He has settled into his enormous selfish loathing. *And you, you love you. And. You. Love. Them. All.* And my robes begin to pulse once more and I am radiant, my wings unfurling about me, brilliant and wide.

# Demon, Right Shoulder

I rub my hands together, one over the other, cold on
his cold shoulder, a shiver runs up my tail and the
knuckles of my spine and I think of the lukewarm response
Master gives when I fail, He always leaves me in the waiting
room—with a worm, a toad, an asp—never opens the door
to the inferno where the flames warm the flesh and the cries
of humans send the spasms through me and I wait and smile
and try a new tack: *You are so sexy when you sit on the far end of the bar,
stirring the bourbon over ice with your fingertip—every woman looks your way,
you charming devil you, the one in the lemon-yellow low-cut number wishes
her man had your lips, they all want to run fingers through your hair, and they
care what you say and even listen to you sing—and every guy, forget it, every
guy wants to sit next to you, listen to your stories and jokes that they will later
tell their friends and pretend they made up. What an interesting life you've led,
pal. Your students just adore your yarns about bar fights and lost weekends in
New Orleans, bootlegging uncles, and the myth of the muse in the rye. Your
inherited birthright is a long tradition built by writers even more gifted than
you, few though they may be: shoot it down, watch college ball, ask the girl in
the wheelchair to dance, shoot an arrow into your ex-wife's front door, buy
guns every chance you get—LeMats, crossbows, dynamite—buy that Sterling
MK6 semiautomatic—you need all that danger a finger's length away because
those fools need something, someone to talk about and that might as well
be you—now it's time to get to work, the computer's buzzing upstairs and the
notebook's blank and the pen's resting cool on your desk and goodness knows
the whole world is waiting to read what you have to write, but first you have to
clear your mind with a drink or two—*

He does not so much as flinch this time, he knows these
lies too well—*Y'know there is no God, don't cha? There is no hell. No*

*Heaven either. Nothing waiting for you after this. This flesh and time is all you have.* I am warmed by his cocked head like a crack in the door, like the heat of the torch set to a martyr. *What I like about you is that you're your own man, the rules don't apply to you and you don't do what people tell you to do,* and he cracks a smile, the crack fissures through his whole body, and he reaches for the bottle and cracks the seal and twists off the top and holds the bottle straight out over the sink and lifts a glass from the counter and I fold my hands together, prayer-wise, and he holds it and holds it still.

## Satan, Eternal, in the Guise of a Bottle
## of Evan Williams Bourbon,
## Ruminating on the Nature of Art, Love, & Life

Please allow me to introduce myself, I am the one
who made this world the way it is—I am sure by now
you will have heard how some other angel forced me from
Heaven—Saint Michael, that arch braggart and blowhard, the
great liar and exaggerator extraordinaire—don't believe a word
of it, kid—I came here willing, this earth is my haven, though
when I first arrived the whole joint was a wreck and you can
trust me when I say Pangaea was all one big chunk of crust, an
island, surrounded by a single body of water—nothing had
been planned, nothing thought all the way through—I took
time and considerable pains to cut runnels for rivers, to carve
craters for lakes and seas, to vary the vegetation and cross-
pollinate and design new breeds because, being the loner
He is, He never dreamt of procreation—His ideas on sex are
laughable, naïve at best—not for animals, not even for trees,
and damn sure not for His people—yeah, yeah, yeah, that
whole "be fruitful and multiply" number was a late edit to the
story, believe you me—I am the one who invented sex, thank
you very much—His plan was for everything to live forever but
all that changed when the first dude ate the fruit and passed it
off on his lady and now even roses and rabbits have to fuck and
die—why? Because misery loves company, because His people
disappointed Him, like He knew they would, like I knew they
would, and He still did it anyway, and that's why I wouldn't
bow before them—but I digress—listen, you seem like a smart

enough guy, a reasonably intelligent guy, let me ask you this:
Does death to everything sound fair? Does that sound like a
reasonable punishment sufficient to fit the crime, the sins of
the father visited not only upon his son but also on his sheep
and lentils?—He didn't think the whole thing through like I
have, even-headed and cool-like—He did not, in fact, even
provide for the full color spectrum—sure, He invented rain,
but I brought the rainbows—before then, there wasn't a speck
of purple on the planet but then I swiped it across horizons so
lovers holding hands could coo and admire my work—instead
they say, *Oh my God, isn't that lovely*—and it is, but not because of
Him, because of me, and they call it the godly color, the royal
color—that's what I do, I bring people together, create spectacles
of love like music—oh yeah, He shuns music, has nothing whatever to do with it, hates it as a cacophony—it makes me laugh
how every time some fool makes a joyful noise unto the Lord,
I can see Him squirm, preparing to send another plague of rats
or brew another violent storm to shut them the hell up, but
I was the current in Jimi's amp, the horn in Armstrong's hands,
the strings on Stravinsky's violin, and I love the baroque as much
as the punk and the women in the woods chanting and banging
sticks onto rocks while Pan teeters on those little goat hooves of
his, eyelashes and flute tunes driving those ladies wild, and
I was there, you know, when the Christians drove them from
the hills, hummocks, and fields deep into caves where they
coiled all manwomanplantandanimal to create a living gro-
tesquery and I've been confused with that guy ever since, as
if I were some puny goat-god, but nahhh, I'm a man-god
maligned by good Christians such as your boy Charlie Daniels
who, I'm here to tell you, is a world-class liar—I've never

even been to Georgia, let alone lost a fiddle match—I was in Mississippi with your Mr. Johnson, and I was his goat hooch laced with strychnine—I was the ale served to kings and their courts during tournaments and the khat in Abel's mouth, the brandy that steadied the artists' hands so they could chisel and paint and pick at the strings; I was the ergot-poisoned wine that turned giants into windmills and windmills into giants and called forth from the deep recesses dragons and mystic visions; I was the fermented fruit in your jailhouse, the rye in your brothels, the vodka in cold tsarist Russia, and the tequila in the teenagers who drive and love carelessly in the summer; I was the scotch in Mr. Dickey's flask at a cockfight outside Macon, Georgia, consoling him after he'd just been kicked off the set of *Deliverance*. I am always here, even now as you and your friends tell stories of duels in the past, how I taught them mean pride and envy and honor and gave them all a false sense of revenge at the tip of the knife, the sword, the bullet, the tongue, and I can teach you as well, because right now, I am only with you, here before your typewriter, your paper, your pens, all laid out before you on your desk, the dim light of an old lamp, the curtains closed, your family asleep. It's just you and me, kid.

Yes, your wife is slated to outlive you by twenty years or more and your son will grow old in his days too, don't fear— I have my eyes on your new lad as well but that's another story yet untold—it doesn't have to be that way. Destiny is not written in stone. Oh no, if you wish for the elixir of immortality then pray listen and I'll tell it true, because I know you want the same things I want—everything this world has to offer and more—you don't have to allow it to dictate to you, son, that's what I'm saying. You have to make of this place what you want. That's what I did. The trouble with you mortals is this: because you can't compare this life with another one, and because you have no chance to revise the one you do get, you are driven into despair and confusion. You all live in doubt, regret, and shame. And why not? You have only this one life to live, or so you think, but I say, leave all of those notions behind—enter the immortals, drink this elixir and know the difference between life and death, between the right way to live and the wrong ways to die, and I'll give you all the chance you will ever need to get it right. Cradle me, swirl me in my bottle, bring me to your mouth and when you're ready to shoot me, bring my lip to your lips, pour me into your mouth, savor the burn, and fire me down your throat, and blow out again and if you do, you will never get drunk, you will never suffer a hangover, and I promise, you will never, ever die.

# Acknowledgments

*Black Warrior Review*: "Pistols at Twenty Paces"

*Faultline*: "Night of the Chicken Run," "A Scalping"

*Juked* (online): "Man above Challenge"

*Louisiana Literature*: "Peleas de Gallo" (as "In the Gallodrome")

*Minnesota Review*: "Into the Greasy Grass"

*New Letters*: "First-Called Quits"

*Nimrod International Journal*: "Fiesta de Semana Santa"

*The Southern Review*: "Custody Battle for Chelsea Tammy"
(as "Custody Battle in the Cabbage Patch")

*storySouth*: "Me and the Devil Blues"

*Surreal South '09*: "On Moses's Failed Insurrection"
(as "On Gabriel's Failed Insurrection")

My unwavering thanks . . .

To my people, for giving me stories to tell;
To Milkweed, for all of your support;
To my FSU family, for shepherding me so well;
To Baldwin Wallace University, for my colleagues and students;

To my Colonel, for leading the charge—hie!
To Doug Cox and Eric Lee, for beer on the patio of LJ's and
the birth of this gun;
To Frank Giampietro, for the long, unflinching eye;
To Ben Barnhart, for giving this book room to run;

To Scott Gage, for tales of brothering;
To Chris Tusa, for older-brothering me;
To Kent Wascom, for younger-brothering me;
To the Drive-By Truckers for providing the soundtrack;

To Jaume, for getting all of this, years from now;
And to Megan, always to Megan, for everything, everything,
everything, everything.

And to all of those I have ignorantly neglected on this page:
You know who you are and how much you mean to me. If you
don't, come by and see me soon, and I'll tell you all about it.
Cheers!

Michael Garriga comes from a long line of Creole outlaws and storytellers. He has worked as a shrimp picker, a bartender, and a soundman in a blues bar. He now teaches writing at Baldwin Wallace University, in Berea, Ohio, where he lives with his wife and two sons. His work has appeared in various journals and magazines. *The Book of Duels* is his first collection of fiction.

Interior design by Connie Kuhnz

Typeset in Mrs Eaves

by BookMobile Design and Digital Publisher Services